Wrapped Up in Us

Kat Ryan

Dedicated to the women out there, forging ahead, even when they are lost in the dark.

And dedicated to those that bring the light.

Chapter 1

Milk Cow

G*race*

My boobs had sprung a leak. I glanced down and saw wet circles that looked kind of like targets appearing before my eyes. Tears threatened, but I was not doing this. I had this. I did. Even when I clearly didn't, I was going to make this work.

"Grace?" Emma, my right hand at the library, walked in, took one look at the girls in my forest-green wrap dress—now marred by the evidence of my overly full breasts—and simply froze. "Oh..."

It was the "oh" that did it. I blame her, because at that word, all the tears that had been threatening to spill over did just that. I dropped my head to my desk and let them roll without restraint.

Unfortunately, the tears made me think of Mia. Thinking of Mia made me miss the little nugget even more. Missing her made said boobs perk up. I think you see where this is going. A trail of dominos. More milk leaked out, emotion flowed, and the circle continued.

I mean, at that point, what did a little more moisture matter in the scheme of things?

Emma closed the door to my office and rushed to my desk, kneeling to the side. "Grace, sweetheart, what can I do?" She smoothed a hand over my blond bob, which used to be smooth and sleek but now was several weeks past when I should have gotten it cut and had seen better days.

The tears increased.

"I am a mess," I moaned.

"Um, well." Emma looked me over like she was debating how to break the news that I was correct in that assumption.

"Emma, I know I am. Look at me!" I pointed at my boobs as Maggie burst through the door.

"Maggie, you should knock," Emma said with a scowl.

Maggie took one look at me and shook her head. "Agree to disagree, my friend. Got here straight from some Mommy and Me with El on my first day of holiday break from the seventh graders. Tim is at the circulation desk and said he heard the telltale sign of tears. I figured time was of the essence."

Emma stood between me and Maggie. Trying to protect me or run from me, I honestly wasn't sure which. "I was just helping Grace. She's feeling a little emotional and—"

Maggie slid around Emma and gave me a once-over. Then she laid out the truth, which was her norm. "Babe, you're a mess."

"I know," I said, wishing I had a Kleenex.

Maggie rustled in her ginormous bag, then handed me exactly that.

"Maggie, I think Grace needs comfort right now and—"

"Emma, no offense, when you pop that kid out in five months, you'll get more where Grace is coming from. Right now, trust me. I know what she needs." Looking back to me, Maggie didn't hesitate. "Okay, lady. First things first, do you have a change of clothes here?"

I nodded, pointing to a bag by the door.

"Got your pump?"

I nodded again, gesturing back to my bag.

"How are you on the modesty scale? Meaning, do you want company while pumping or want us to set it up and give you some privacy?"

"We would stay in here while she was *pumping?*" Emma was aghast, but then she shot me a wink to let me know she was at least half joking. A few months ago, I would have been with her. However, upon becoming a milk cow, I'd lost some of my give-a-shits.

Maggie rolled her eyes. "I mean, I'm just offering, and you've been with me a million times while I've pumped. Grace is clearly on edge. If she doesn't want to be alone, it's not like we don't have breasts. And I've pumped and you will be in a few months, so..."

Emma's reaction served its purpose—it snapped me out of my emotions. "Sorry. I'm doing better." I sniffed. "To answer your question, not too modest, but I think I'm okay to go it alone. No need to traumatize Emma today."

Maggie looked me over like she'd make her own judgment. "Hmm, okay. You are looking calmer. How about we help you get set up, and then we'll meet you down in the kitchen when you're done?"

Within minutes, I was hooked up to my Medela and the familiar suction began to provide relief even while it pissed me off. Maggie had set up my phone on my desk so I could binge an episode or two as I sat there in the office on the second floor of the Ryan Library, doing the work that new moms everywhere did as they returned after maternity leave.

What a crock.

Half an hour and one dress change later, with double pads this time in my nursing bra, I headed downstairs and into the kitchen to find Maggie and Emma and the scent of fresh-baked cookies in the air. Tim, one of our other librarians, must have decided to give us some privacy and work in the main part of the library, which was, if you knew him, shocking.

This library was home. I'd missed it in the past three months while on maternity leave. I hadn't grown up in Highland Falls. Neither had Aidan, my husband, but when I first visited this public library during college, I fell in love. Two sisters had left their colonial revival home to the town a century ago, and the town turned it into the library. Newer libraries would have more modern conveniences, but I loved this space. The oak woodwork, lead glass windows, quirky rooms—it all spoke to my heart. Upon entering the library, you walked up to the circulation desk in the former foyer. The stairs took you up to our offices, the conference room, and storage. Downstairs we had kids' books, children, and young adult to the left of the foyer; fiction and nonfiction to the right. All roads led you to the back of the house where the kitchen stood as a staff break room and a place to cook with patrons when we hosted various book clubs. They were also welcome to coffee. Several had their own special mugs they left here. Tables and comfy chairs dotted the entire place, making this everything I wanted in a library and more.

Maggie and Emma pushed a tray of warm chocolate chip cookies in my direction. I snatched one up and inhaled it.

Maggie slid a mug of coffee toward me, and I gave her an assessing glance.

"Decaf" was her response.

I reverently took a sip.

"Okay, lady, sit." Maggie nodded to the couch in the window area of the kitchen. "You've been telling us everything is great. But Grace, you have a three-month-old kid and you are on day two back from maternity leave, hopping into your role as director of this library. There is no such thing as 'great' at this stage."

Tears welled up again. I cursed my postpartum hormones. Could I still blame them three months out?

"I don't want to be ungrateful," I said in a voice I didn't even recognize. Damn it. One year ago, I was in charge. I had been rattled, I'll admit, that it took us more than one month to conceive, which I knew was ridiculous. I'd been— no, we'd been—naive. Aidan and I spent the first ten plus years of our marriage actively trying to *prevent* pregnancy. We'd thought that as soon as we wanted to have a baby, it would happen. Nope. After months of trying, we sought help. The doctors assured us that we were fine and to relax and let it happen in time.

Telling someone to relax was like telling them not to worry when they were anxious.

We were, however, some of the lucky ones. I hated that other couples struggled to conceive. Ten months in, we got the long-awaited second line. My pregnancy had been relatively easy other than my husband being a nervous wreck and wanting to keep me in bed where nothing could happen to me, especially in the final months. Our labor and delivery hit a few speed bumps, and the cesarean section hadn't been planned, but Mia was here, she was healthy, and I felt like an ass if I complained about anything.

Maggie and Emma followed me to the couch under the windows in the kitchen. I curled up in one corner while the other two faced me and seemed to consider my words.

Maggie was the first to speak, which pretty much defined her personality. "Why are you ungrateful?"

I gestured with my hand that wasn't holding the coffee cup. "You know, we were lucky enough to get pregnant, I have a healthy baby, a doting husband, blah, blah, blah."

The two women I considered close friends blinked at me. Repeatedly.

"But Grace, just because that's true doesn't mean you've lost the right to complain about anything." Emma looked confused.

I sat with that.

Maggie pulled out her phone. "I have an idea. I'm going to set the timer on here for two minutes. You have that time to complain about anything you want, and we swear we won't judge you; it won't make you a bad person, and you'll feel better getting it out. You with me?"

"Two minutes? Sure." No idea what that would accomplish, but I was willing to try.

"Okay, while I find the timer, do some preplanning like I tell my seventh graders. Think of what you're going to say so you can hit the ground running and get it all out."

I nodded, considering what I wanted, or needed, to say.

"Okay. Three, two, one—lay it on us." Maggie hit some button on her phone.

I took a breath and then poured it all out. "I haven't slept more than four hours in a row for three months. My boobs hurt." Just saying that made them ache, and I fought the urge to cup each breast. "All the time. My C-section scar is ugly, and I feel like there is a shelf of belly over it that will never be remotely flat again." I gestured in the direction of said shelf. "Mia's poor little tummy is gassy, which makes her cry a lot. Only pressure on her stomach makes her stop crying sometimes. She needs to be touching Aidan or me at all times, which is sweet but makes me feel touched out, like I need space, which makes me feel like a bitch."

I thought about my life before Mia and now. "I feel like I'm losing my identity. Like I was an interesting person before having a baby, but now I feel like I'm Mia's mom first and everything else is secondary, if even considered. I never realized that nursing meant I either need to be available to feed her every few hours or pump if we aren't together, even if it's one of the only things I think I'm doing well. It's like in having a baby, I lost any time for just me, which is, again, selfish. Not to mention, nursing *hurt* at first, like bleeding-nipples-split-in-two hurts." My body winced on its own, remembering those first days and weeks.

I let out a deep breath and continued. "I feel like a ball of emotions that isn't deflating. Anything and everything can set me off. The other day I cried because I thought Baxter felt neglected, which meant I was a horrible mother." Tears streamed down as I grabbed a Kleenex and blew my nose.

I saw Maggie look toward Emma. "Baxter?"

"The corgi," Emma replied.

Maggie raised an eyebrow at me in disbelief. "Setting aside the notion of the dog being neglected, how does that make you a horrible mom?"

"He was my first child." I dropped my head to the back of the couch.

Emma leaned over and rubbed my shoulder. "Grace, you know that's not true. You're a great mom—to Mia *and* Baxter."

Then I thought of Aidan. He'd been curled up in bed

this morning with Mia when I left for work. "And with Aidan…" I hesitated, then confessed my biggest concerns. "I worry that we're drifting apart because we're never alone anymore. I don't think he thinks I'm sexy, that he only sees me as a dairy farm. And I'm afraid we'll never have sex again." I thought about it, then looked at the girls. "That's it."

Maggie tapped her phone and held it up to me. "You didn't even fill up two minutes."

Strangely, I did feel a bit better, like I wasn't alone in this.

"But we are talking about your concerns because, Grace, those are all completely normal feelings."

"Really?"

"Really. Well, the dog one might be a bit much." She grinned and me, then held up a finger. "One—and listen up, Emma, because this will be your life come summer…"

Emma put a hand on her small belly.

"So, one, Mia will sleep at some point. I promise. Can either Aidan's mom or yours take Mia for the night? One good night of sleep for you is huge. Lee and Anna took El for us once every other week starting at about a month. I'm not overstating it when I say that it was life changing."

Lee and Anna Sullivan were the amazing parents of Emma and her brother, Cole Sullivan, aka Sully, Maggie's husband. My parents weren't terrible people, but I couldn't see them volunteering for duty. Aidan's mom was amazing, yet I hadn't even considered asking her to drive down, though I was sure she would. The logistics just made me a bit crazy.

"How did you do that? Overnights? You were nursing too."

"Bottles, babe. Pump and prepare."

"I mean, I know, but part of me feels like that's cheating, like I need to be doing it all. I have no choice but to pump at work, but at night? Will that mess with our attachment?"

"Nope. No way, no how. The bullshit version of motherhood where we have to martyr ourselves needs to go. Get rid of it. The long and short of it is it gets easier with time and when you don't try to do it all. But let's get to point two —you feeling unattractive. You said you and Aidan haven't had sex for some time. Since Mia was born, I'm guessing?"

My gut clenched, and a feeling of guilt welled up inside. "Since I hit around thirty-six weeks actually. I was nervous because we had an issue with spotting."

"So about four months? I'd say it's time for that drought to end. You *will* feel sexier once you see how Aidan reacts to you." Maggie wagged her eyebrows, and Emma hit her in the arm.

"I don't know, ladies. I mean, between my body by the end of pregnancy, the C-section, nursing, leaking, stretch marks, the weird belly I have now... I just feel like all the sexy parts of me are gone and he isn't attracted to me anymore. Are we going to become one of those couples that are just friends and sexy times are a distant memory?"

"Grace-alicious." The man of the hour strolled in, making my face flame, and I prayed he hadn't overheard anything. Aidan Russo had made my mouth water when we were sophomores in college at the University of Illinois, and not much had changed in the past sixteen years. His dark hair was longer on top than it had been back then, more tousled. His face was rarely clean-shaven, but his scruff wasn't to the levels of a thick beard.

One addition that was certainly not with him when we met was our daughter, Mia. She'd turned three months old this weekend and was currently strapped to his chest in a sling and clearly down for the count. My return from maternity leave this week meant Aidan was taking over at home. He was staying home for another month, taking a paternity leave from his role as a deputy at our county's sheriff's department. After that, Mia would be headed to an in-home daycare here in town.

Aidan came by and kissed my head, then handed me my lunch bag. "You forgot this, so I figured I'd pop by and drop it off."

"Thanks," I murmured, also kissing the top of Mia's head before glancing down to see if my boobs were responding to the sight of my child. Dry so far. Yay? "She good?"

"Yep, an angel." He smiled, then gave me a second glance, concern marring his expression. "You okay?" He traced a thumb across my cheek.

"Hormones." One word was a whole statement.

His gaze grew focused. "How can I help?"

I shook my head, then gestured to the cookies at the table. "Maggie and Emma are taking care of me."

He watched me for another moment, shook his head, then looked to Maggie and Emma. "You two doing okay? Causing any trouble?"

"You know it," Maggie said, doing a little shimmy on the couch.

"I'm off to meet the guys for lunch at the Homestead," Aidan said. "Anything you need, Grace? I can stay here if it would help."

"No, I'm truly fine." I scanned his face, looking for any indications of hesitation. "You're really headed to the brewery? What if she gets fussy?"

He shrugged. "I've got a bottle and diapers. And if she cries, it won't be the first time people have heard a baby get a little upset. I figure we'll just roll with it." He leaned over again, pressing another kiss to my forehead. "See you at home. We can talk more there." And with that he headed out the door.

I looked back at Maggie and Emma, trying to work out the emotions running rampant inside me.

Emma took the chance to give my leg a sympathetic squeeze. "We'll figure it out, Grace. Aidan loves you; that's clear."

I nodded. I knew he loved me, but something was missing, and I didn't know how to fix it.

"At least while we figure it out, we can all appreciate your gorgeous husband, who has zero reservation about walking around with a baby strapped to him. Because that just makes his hotness factor skyrocket, am I right?" Maggie was nothing if not blunt.

Tim appeared and leaned against the doorway to the kitchen. "Girl, you are so right. I had to fan myself when that hot hunk of man walked in here with little Mia on his chest." Tim was apparently done with giving us privacy. "So what's up with this dry spell I overheard you talking about, and how can we get you some action?"

Palm to the forehead. The last thing I needed right that minute was Tim. But the man did have a good point.

Chapter 2

Dad on Duty

A*idan*

Walking into the Homestead, I scanned the bar for the guys. Mia shifted in the sling, and I patted her little butt as I moved through the crowd, using my arm to protect her from anyone who might inadvertently bump into her.

My mind jumped from Grace's face at the library, to the way she'd been acting of late, to my growling stomach and desire to devour some food. I couldn't think on an empty stomach. Time to remedy that. Maybe the guys would be able to help me sort out what was going on with my Gracie.

A look to my left gave me a Maxwell Harp sighting. With a quick turn, I was headed into the bar area. It was lunchtime, so it wasn't like anyone was bellied up and having too many. No. Instead, a low table on the side with an assortment of soft armchairs was taken up by Cole Sullivan and his and Maggie's daughter, Ellen. El was turning a year any day now. Sully had her plopped into a high chair with a container of Cheerios, which El seemed to enjoy pounding on the table rather than eating any.

Next to El on a bench was Addie, Jake's stepdaughter with Ivy. Jake was nearby, keeping an eye on her and El, but Addie was five and pretty self-sufficient. She was stacking the Cheerios that were being scattered by El into little towers, much to El's delight.

"Gahhhh." El laughed and smashed her hand on another tower, which had the chain reaction of making Addie laugh as she looked to Jake.

"Daddy Two, I can make her smile."

"You sure can, peanut." Jake looked her way with clear affection on his face.

I'd known Jake and Sully since they began working on this place years ago. Max I'd met when he moved home a year and a half ago. He joined us by pulling up a chair at the end of the table next to Sully. I noted Drew and Logan on the couch across from the bench at the table. Those two were more recent friends. In the past few years, they'd all paired off, found their happy-ever-afters.

And now babies were booming. Max and Emma were having a baby in May, Allyson and Logan had just announced they were having one in June, and Jake and Ivy had just had baby Lorelai two weeks ago, which likely explained why Jake was joining us with Addie, who was on the first day of her break from kindergarten, giving Ivy a moment of peace with the baby at home.

Our group had grown and then some.

"Maybe we need a dad's playgroup," I said as I lowered myself and Mia to the armchair at the other end of the table.

"No babies for us yet," Drew said of himself and his wife, Kate, "but I'd be down to hang with yours anytime."

"You're pretty much a kid yourself," Jake said with a look across the table at his brother.

Drew shrugged, not seeming to disagree. "Hey, Ads," he

said, leaning across the table to talk to his niece, "want to do my nails?"

Addie quickly turned and grabbed a bag of nail polish that Jake had sitting beside him as Drew placed his hands on the table so that she could reach. The girl loved painting nails. Jake had said she'd asked her teacher if she could make it a center at school and they'd said yes. Apparently she'd started with Jake and Drew. The two men often sported painted nails when they visited her classroom. As a result, boys and girls alike lined up to be Addie's next customers.

Daryl was bartending and came over to take the table's lunch order.

When Daryl finished, Sully looked around the table, then met my gaze. "Russo, how's the dad gig going?"

I shrugged as I reached over to put a bottle on the table for easy access when Mia made it known it was time to eat. "Seems good so far." I held back, not sure what Grace would want me to share, though I was certain she didn't hold much back with Maggie and Emma. Unfortunately, the same couldn't be said with me. In all fairness, I'd not been speaking up much either.

"And you and Grace are settling into life as parents?" he asked as he seemed to search my face. For what, I had no idea. "No setbacks?"

My gut tightened. We were doing as well as could be expected for new parents, weren't we? I felt judged in a way I wasn't in love with. Instead of examining that, I decided to answer Sully.

"I mean, yeah? I'm tired. Hell, I know Grace is too, but isn't that pretty typical of new parents? No one promised a baby who came out and enjoyed a solid eight hours." I shrugged away any concern as I continued to rub Mia's back. She should be waking up anytime now, and I didn't want to get her off schedule.

Sully seemed to be holding back as he looked at me with a calculating glance.

I debated letting it go, not really wanting to delve too deep, but honestly, the lack of sleep had robbed me of a filter. "Spill, man. What?"

Sully leaned back, the picture of ease as he laid out truth bombs. "Just saying if you two are settling smoothly into the life of parents, you are a unicorn of a couple."

I replayed his words, wondering if they'd make more sense a second time. "A unicorn couple?"

Drew muttered to the table, "Wasn't aware we were going to be discussing Russo's horn."

"Watch it," Jake growled with a nod toward Addie. She was engrossed in her manicure and hadn't clued into Drew's comment.

Sully cleared his throat, pulling my attention back to him. "What I mean is that I don't know many that had smooth sailing moving from being a married couple to parents." He looked to Jake. "Agreed?"

Jake shifted focus from where he'd been straightening Addie's nail polish to lock eyes with Sully. "Smooth sailing in becoming a parent?" he asked, confirming our current debate.

"Yeah." Sully tilted his head toward Addie. "How was your adjustment from zero to one, or the more recent shift from one to two?"

Jake sat back, appearing to consider his words. "I mean, Ads was four when I came on the scene, so I'm not sure that one is a fair comparison. I don't know a relationship with

Ivy without the peanut. Though it was still an adjustment, but one I was consumed by." He rubbed a hand over his face, lost in thought with a slight grin before looking more serious. "Now, the past two weeks has been something else."

Sully and I nodded, commiserating. Sleep deprivation was no joke. No wonder some assholes used it as a method of torture. I'd been so grateful when Mia started having a three-hour stretch in the middle of the night where she slept. It wasn't enough, but it had been huge.

"Mommy was mad at Daddy Two this morning," Addie said, not looking up from her job polishing Drew's nails. I noted that she was alternating red and green on his fingers. A holiday feel. Nice.

Drew, as the consummate younger brother, didn't let that comment go unnoticed. "Daddy Two irritated Bookstore, did he? Not surprising."

Drew had called Ivy "Bookstore" since they'd met, something all of us, including Addie apparently, just rolled with at this point.

"Yep," Addie said as she switched colors once again. "Mommy said he needed to get his hearing checked." With that, she focused, picking up Drew's pinkie finger and concentrating on the job at hand. Her tongue poked out of her mouth, and her brow furrowed.

The rest of us, on the other hand, had no such task in front of us, so we all turned toward Jake, who had a flush working its way up his cheeks.

"Need to go shopping for hearing aids, big bro?" Drew said, leaning into the teasing.

Jake looked from one of us to another, then tossed his arms up in defeat. "I'm not proud, guys, but in my defense, I was really tired. Like I didn't know my name tired."

"Do tell." Drew's eyes gleamed.

Jake said something so fast I didn't catch it, and then he grabbed his beer and took a gulp.

"I'm sorry, did you just say that you pretended to be asleep so Bookstore would have to get up with Lorelai, your two-week-old baby?" Drew looked aghast, which was likely partly true, and somewhat a bit of acting to make his brother feel worse.

Was it wrong to be happy my brother wasn't local?

Jake braced his elbows on the table and slumped forward, looking miserable. "I know, I know. And Ivy has been nursing through the nights, and she's such a rock star. I feel horrible, and yet it's like I'm not going to make it without some sleep soon. So I thought if I just lay quietly, Lorelai would go back to sleep. But Ivy got up, then saw me peeking or something—the woman just *knew* I was faking..."

"And how did that go over?" Max spoke up.

"Not well."

"You better hope like hell that Bookstore doesn't pass this info on to Steph," Drew murmured, referencing their older sister.

We all winced, knowing the oldest Spencer sibling from her trips to Highland. She was not to be messed with, and Jake should probably fear for his life.

The table was quiet, and I had no idea what they all were thinking about, but I knew what was on my mind and I had to speak up.

"Been there, man."

"Oh, you poor bastard." Max shook his head with pity. "Did Grace catch you?"

I nodded with regret.

"You'll be lucky if she's open for spicy times anytime soon," Max said with a chuckle.

"I'm sorry, 'spicy times'?" Sully said, looking at his oldest friend, not about to let that one slide.

Max raised a middle finger in Sully's direction as he subtly scratched his nose with it. "Emma's always talking about spice levels of romance books. I like it." Max took a sip of his beer.

"Bet she is." Drew raised a brow.

Logan, sitting next to him, shoved him. Luckily it wasn't too hard or the manicure could have suffered.

"What spicy times?" I kept my eyes locked on my beer, not wanting to meet anyone's sympathetic gaze but figuring it was time to talk about this. I didn't know who else to turn to.

The silence that my statement was met with, however, made me look up to see the eyes of five men drilling into me. I felt my face heat. Had I overstepped? I mean, we joked around a lot. I'd known Jake and Sully for over five years. Even with the more recent additions of the other guys, I knew I could trust them, but it wasn't like we had deep, heartfelt, and vulnerable conversations often. But honestly, I had to figure this out, and I couldn't lay my insecurities on Grace. She was under enough pressure.

Jake cleared his throat, then gave me a look of encouragement. "Aidan, I'm going to speak for these Neanderthals that we're both lucky enough to call friends. How can we help?"

I focused on patting Mia's little bum as I placed a kiss to her head and tried to get my thoughts organized. "It's just... I mean, it's been... But then I feel so selfish... And she's so amazing I'm in awe..."

"Hold on." Sully interrupted whatever I was trying to say.

I looked up and realized he hadn't just been providing

me relief—Daryl and Laurie were headed over with our food.

The next few minutes were a flurry of activity as plates were passed around and Jake got Addie set up with chicken tenders along with mac and cheese. Drew blew on his nails to dry them, and Daryl brought over a few beers. Sully got El started with some cut-up grapes and hot dogs, and Jake passed some coloring sheets to Addie. Just as I thought my verbal diarrhea might have been forgotten, Sully got the conversation back on track.

"Aidan, I'm just going to put this out there because it might be easier for you if we dive in. I'm guessing it has been a while since"—he glanced to Addie, then back to me—"any spicy times have happened at Casa de la Russo? Is that a fair statement?"

"Nothing fair, or fun, about that, man," Drew said quietly.

Logan tapped his glass to Drew's.

"Are we saying 'a while' as in"—Max looked at Mia with a tilt of his head—"about twelve weeks?"

"Bit longer," I muttered. "Maybe four months? End of pregnancy was rough."

"Damn," Max muttered.

Logan and Drew nodded in commiseration.

"Come on." Jake shook his head at the table. "All of you have gone at least four months without"—his eyes shot to Addie—"*spicy times*. It's not the end of the world, though it does suck, man."

"Agreed," I murmured. "It's not the time so much. More like I love Gracie and she's right there, but she's not. I know she felt like shit that last four weeks before this peanut arrived. And now she's just doing so much. Nursing alone is such a toll on her body. Well, and…" My voice trailed off, and I felt all eyes on me.

Logan finally broke the silence. "You're still attracted to her, right?"

"Of course I am. I mean, have you seen my wife?" My face was on fire.

Logan put up his hands. "No offense, man, just thought I'd ask and get that out there. So who's holding back?"

I slid back in the chair. I wished I could say it was all Grace, but that was bullshit. "I mean, I think we both are? I can't speak for her, but after watching her go through all that at the end, I feel like I'm going to hurt her, which would kill me. And honestly, I don't feel like she misses it."

Sully nodded at me from the other end of the table. "I get where you're coming from, man, I absolutely do. Birth is no joke, and I know Grace had a C-section, which is another level of hell. So I get you, and Maggie is going to be so damn proud of me for asking this, but have you talked to Grace about it?"

I groaned, sinking down in the armchair with my arm around the sling and Mia. "No. I just feel so stupid. Am I overreacting? Maybe this is the way it's supposed to be, and I'm just some horny man who needs to back way the heck off."

Sully shook his head as he reached over and tugged El out of the high chair, plopping her on his lap. He wiped her hands clean of any lunch residue and handed her a sippy cup, scooting down in the chair so she could settle her body against his. Sully kissed the top of her head and then met my gaze. "Not overreacting man, but clearly there is something there you two need to discuss. Who knows, she might be struggling with this too."

I let out a breath, my heart aching at the thought of my

Grace struggling with anything. All I wanted to do was protect her from... Hell, everything? Maybe that even included me? Jesus.

Mia began squirming against me, announcing the end of her nap and this conversation. That was fine—I had a lot to think about.

Chapter 3

Corgi Love

race
Every fiber of my being ached. I'd thought I was being so smart, scheduling my first week back from maternity leave to be a shorter one. Get in, get out, have a weekend to recoup, then another short week due to the Christmas holiday. I hadn't counted on some of our part-time folks being out sick and my being needed for story hour. I'd also forgotten we had a holiday open house scheduled for the community on Sunday. So yeah, I'd *thought* I was being smart, but in reality, I was dragging. So dang tired, and the walk home had been a bleary one.

Despite the cold, I loved the fact that we lived close enough for me to walk to work. Even with a light covering of snow on the ground, the crisp air attempted to pull me out of this exhaustion. The bare trees were sentries lining the road as I dug my hands deeper in the pockets of my parka, quickening my steps as I made my way down the rapidly darkening street.

The Ryan Library was just off the downtown area of

Highland Falls where many of the oldest homes in town had been built. Aidan and I had purchased our house two years after moving here once out of college. When I landed the job as library director in Highland, he got a job with the sheriff's department since he couldn't find a local position using his degree in communications. We'd rented for two years while we saved up for a down payment while conversely bleeding money to pay off our student loans, much like young adults everywhere. Luckily, we were both focused and agreed to hunker down and save as much as we could, living like hermits. Eating out, traveling, buying anything "fun"—all were extravagances we couldn't afford.

Fast-forward two years, and we had a small nest egg with dwindling loans. As luck would have it, a bungalow had come on the market. For certain, it needed work, which meant we could afford it. We got it, and the house became our new focus with small projects we could tackle on our own or, once Aidan became friends with Jake and Sully, with their added help. Now it was my dream home with a farmhouse vibe, just right for our small family and Baxter the wonder corgi.

My heart rate used to pick up the closer I got to home. I was anxious to see Aidan, to spend time with my best friend, to soak in the comfort I felt in my skin when we were together. Years into this relationship, looking back, it felt like we were babies when it all began. Aidan knew me better than anyone, or at least he used to.

The guilt I had in not confiding where my mind had been for the past few months or, heck, the past year, was tremendous. But there was a large part of me that felt like a failure. Would Aidan judge me if I shared? Two years ago, I would have said no. Now? In all honesty, I judged myself.

Motherhood looked so easy on other people. What was wrong with me that I couldn't adapt like Maggie or anyone else?

As I reached our porch, I admired the holiday feel. Aidan had strung some white lights along the evergreen swag above the trim and on the two smaller evergreens I'd put on either side of our black front door. Home. While I wasn't feeling myself, I did feel like I'd reached my safe haven.

"I'm home," I called as I stepped into the house.

"Back here."

Leaning to one side, I tugged off one tall boot before doing the same to the other. I wiggled my toes in relief and then looked at the staircase in front of me where Baxter, our sweet pup, was bouncing down the steps, butt wagging.

He reached the bottom and leaned his little body against my legs, getting his glitter, aka corgi hair, all over my knee-high socks.

"Hey, puppers," I cooed, leaning down to rub my hand over his back. "Let's go find Dad and Mia."

Baxter's ears perked up, and he trotted down the short hall to the open kitchen and family room space that lined the back of our home, rubbing his body against the wall the whole way there. I shook my head, noting the streaks of dirt on the wall from the repeated action, but then stopped at the end of the hall, taking in the beautiful sight in front of us.

Aidan and Mia were in the kitchen with Mia strapped into the sling. She was alert though, her head poking out with an adorable Santa hat that I hadn't seen before. Mia was cooing as Aidan swayed around the open space, singing along to some song that I could hear coming from the speaker on the counter. Noah Kahan, if I wasn't mistaken. Hmm. "Call Your Mom" was a pretty emotional one, but I could get behind the sentiment.

Watching Aidan swing around our kitchen with Mia hit my emotions more than I'd been prepared for. I saw the man I loved, had loved for so many years, and he was killing it as a dad. He was so natural with her; I was jealous, and I hated that.

I leaned my hip against the wall to watch, love filling me up inside as I worked to push away the green-eyed monster. Aidan swayed with a hand on Mia's little tush, his eyes closed as he moved through the space around the island, singing to her. Mia's eyes were locked on his, entranced.

While I saw him as the man he was, I also saw the nineteen-year-old boy I'd bumped into at the graduate library so many years ago. I'd been melting down as I tried to get a paper written while I was sicker than a dog. Aidan had seen the tears of a complete stranger and immediately stepped in to help me, offering solutions that snapped me out of my spiral, something he clearly hadn't needed to do. But that was Aidan—if he could help, even a stranger, he would. It's why he was good at his job. Not much rattled him, his heart was pure, and he operated on a level of low stress that I envied with everything in me.

I looked beyond them to the view of our backyard. The sun had long set and it was dark. A few more months and five p.m. wouldn't look like midnight, but for now... The winter days were long. The windows became mirrors at this time of day, and I caught Aidan's gaze in the glass.

"Hey, babe, we missed you today," he said to me in the window's reflection, shooting me a wink.

I shook my head at the man, who exuded the confidence

I wished I could resurrect as I moved to greet him and Mia with a kiss.

"Did you have a good day?" I asked, pulling Mia out and cradling her to me, tugging the Santa hat off and laying it on the counter. Mia cooed as I breathed her scent deep, soaking in the solid feeling of my baby in my arms.

The irony of motherhood was that I missed her all day long like a limb had been severed from my body *and* I had zero desire to stay home even if we had been able to swing it. I hadn't realized how much I missed work until I went back, and even as tired as I was, it was as if my brain was lit up with new ideas after flatlining for months. How was it that I could love this child more than my life while also absolutely needing to work outside the home? The guilt of it ate me up inside. Thank God we'd found a terrific in-home daycare for her to start at next month after Aidan's leave was over. Praying to the gods above that it would help ease some of it.

Aidan turned to the Crock-Pot on the counter, grabbing a potato masher he often used to quickly shred chicken after cooking it all day. He looked in my direction as he lifted the lid. "I'll answer that after you make a choice—tacos or burrito bowls?"

"Do we have avocados for guac?"

He raised a brow in my direction. "Am I my mother's son?"

"Cilantro rice?"

He shook his head in mock disappointment. "It's like you don't even know me."

"Bowls please." I moved to the couch in our family room, sitting on the section where I could still see Aidan working on dinner. I tamped down the feeling that I should tell Aidan to take a break because he'd been with the baby all day. I knew he'd tell me he was fine and to park myself right where I was.

"So how was she?" I asked, putting my feet on the coffee table and leaning Mia back against my thighs so I could bicycle her little legs.

Aidan didn't look up from his food prep as he answered. "Great all day; started getting cranky just before five."

"In other words, the usual," I said, working to get a smile from our gassy little girl. For her first month, anytime from five to seven in the evening was pure hell on earth. She'd scream no matter what we did, and I felt like a failure. Lately she just got fussy, and I was grateful for it.

Aidan laughed from the stove where he was stirring some rice. "Exactly."

"Last bottle?"

"A little after two," he said with a glance toward the clock. At a quarter past five, that meant I was up.

I pulled Mia toward me and slid back to the corner of the couch, grabbing pillows to support the two of us as she nursed. Once I got her situated, she started smacking her lips, knowing where this little dance was headed.

Nursing had been hell at first. I couldn't say why I'd stuck with it—I strongly believed formula was absolutely fine and didn't buy into the idea that nursing made you a better mother or the pressure that society put on women. There was just something inside me that really wanted it to work. And thus, through much trial and error, we were finally at this place where it was a moment with my baby that I loved.

Some days nursing felt like the only thing I was doing *well*, even though it was still a pain in the butt to pump and leaking was the bane of my existence. But this? These moments where Mia would curl her little body around my waist and one tiny hand would almost pat my side as if to say *good job, Mama?* Yeah, I lived for it.

Mia's rhythmic sucking and the low music had me feeling sleepy as I snuggled deeper into the couch, unwinding from the day. Typically Mia nursed at both sides each feeding and, sure enough, I felt her getting restless when she was ready to switch. By almost rote memory at this point, I reached down to help her unlatch. We did a quick burp before resuming on the other side. Once she was settled, I looked up to see Aidan's gaze on the two of us from the kitchen island.

I looked down at myself and felt as unsexy as I'd ever been. The wrap dress and nursing bra were convenient, sure. You could just tug down and access what was needed without much work. But it only lent to the feeling of frumpiness I was struggling with. Heck, I felt splayed out here—wet boob, milk smeared around. I'm sure I was a vision. No wonder Aidan hadn't seemed interested in sex. Who would?

"She out?" Aidan asked as he pulled down the bowls for dinner, making me wonder if he'd even noticed my lack of sex appeal of late.

I glanced down at Mia, running my finger over her cheek. Her brown eyes popped open, locking on mine. They'd been blue-gray at birth, and I'd wondered if my blue eyes could hold strong against Aidan's brown ones, but no go. Then again, it had been years since I'd learned about recessive and dominant genes, but I knew mine weren't as strong as his. His brown hair had already won the battle over my blond, not that Mia had much to write home about yet.

"Nope, still with us," I replied as she gave me a milky smile. Good Lord, I felt that one in my soul.

"Want me to dish your food up for you?" Aidan said as he pulled together the last bit of our meal.

My mouth watered when the spicy scent from the chicken hit me. "Sure."

Aidan made quick work of assembling our burrito bowls, then came over to the couch and set up an activity mat we'd gotten at one of our showers. It had toys and a mirror arcing over Mia while she lay on her back, and she'd kick and wave her arms, knocking into toys and fortunately entertaining herself long enough for us to eat a meal together.

Aidan took Mia from me and slid her under the toys as I got myself back together. He handed me a bowl from the coffee table as he sank onto the couch with me, both of us in opposite corners, Mia just a step away.

I took a bite and sent my gratitude out to Aidan's mom, Sophia. Not only was she amazing to the point that I was closer to her than my own mom, she was also a fabulous cook and had taught both her boys to take after her. Then again, Aidan and his brother Declan had lost their dad, Joe, when Aidan was ten and Declan was eight. I knew Aidan had stepped up into a caretaker role at that point, as much as Sophia tried to stop him and get him to be a kid.

Heck, clearly, he was still living that role. At this point, I figured it was part of his DNA.

Looking his way, I gave a soft smile to my guy. I still loved him even though I was seriously wondering when, if ever, we'd get back to who we were. He was just so *good*. Like a darn golden retriever. Loyal and true.

"This is delicious, babe."

"Thanks," he said, then kicked a gift bag on the coffee table that I had somehow missed. "Ben stopped by today."

Ben was a deputy at the sheriff's department with Aidan.

"And he brought a gift?"

"It's from the guys."

I considered the gift bag. It was Christmas themed with red and green tissue paper sticking out of the top. "Did you open it?"

"Wanted to wait for you." Aidan nodded toward the bag. "Go ahead."

"You don't want to open it? It's from your coworkers."

"Nah."

I set my bowl aside and grabbed the bag, tugging out the tissue paper and peering inside. I saw some holiday fabric and pulled it out, spreading both items on my lap.

Oh. My. Goodness.

There was a sling, pink with little Christmas trees on it in various shades of pink and purple, and then there was a matching sweater for Baxter.

Aidan immediately chuckled, calling Baxter and holding the sweater open for our pup. It was insane, but Baxter actually liked wearing sweaters and would tunnel through, kicking his little legs to get them in the armholes.

He did just that, and it was a perfect fit.

Aidan leaned over and grabbed his phone from his pocket before taking a pic of our adorable pup. "I'll just send this to the guys and tell them thanks."

I nodded, running my hand over the sling. I loved that I knew Aidan would have no issue walking around town in a pink sling. Toxic masculinity had no space in his head to the point his coworkers knew it.

I was so attracted to him, but at the same time, zero

desire was bubbling up inside me. I didn't know how to talk about it without feeling like I was rejecting him. Damn.

"You done, babe?" He was standing up, holding out a hand for my plate.

"Aidan, you've done so much. How about I clean up?" My heart was hammering like I was worried about something. What was that?

Instead of saying anything, he knelt to press a kiss to my head. "Babe, you worked a full day, and as soon as you got home, you nursed our baby, which is another full-time job. You need to have some downtime. I haven't forgotten the way you looked when we got to the library today."

My heart pounded more. "I was just tired."

He bopped my nose with his finger. "Um-hm." Standing up, he nodded to Mia. "Hang with her for a few minutes, spend some time together before bed, then we can divide and conquer. You can nurse her one last time and I'll get a bath ready for you, then I'll get her down while you get a good soak and relax."

My face flamed, which I would like to note had never been an issue for me before in life, but damn did I feel like I wasn't pulling my own weight. "You're doing everything."

Aidan bent over, tucked my hair behind my ear, and whispered, "When are you going to clue into the fact that I love taking care of you?"

With that, he stood up, taking my dish and heading to the kitchen while I slid to the floor to stretch out by Mia, feeling like one more item on the Aidan Russo to-do list.

* * *

The bath was the perfect temperature as I sank into the water. Guilt gnawed at me as I thought of Aidan laying Mia down to bed. Fingers crossed she'd be easy and would go down and stay down for the next four hours. While my husband and I might be operating right now more as friends than romantic partners, I was ashamed that he was carrying so much of the parental load at the moment. He'd had Mia all day, made dinner, and now was putting her down so I could wind down in a bath? When I was home for the first three months, it was a dang miracle if I was showered every other day.

My inner voice reminded me that she'd slept even less consecutively as a newborn, and I should cut myself a break.

I grabbed a soap that I'd picked up at the gift shop in town and ran it over my skin. The lavender was heady, and my breathing evened out as I finally found it in me to relax. I ran the suds over one arm, across my breasts, and then down the other arm. I willed myself to feel sexual, to have any desire come up.

Instead, I yawned. No, I was not going to bed before Aidan was done with Mia. Maybe, just maybe, if I could stay awake until he was in the room, we could at least kiss. It was better than nothing, right?

As I rinsed the soap off, I realized I couldn't soak in here like Aidan had suggested. It was a nice thought, but I was at risk of falling asleep in the bath, and that just seemed dangerous and contrary to my plan.

Instead, I finished up and quickly got out of the tub, moving through my nightly routine, drying off and applying lotion, brushing through my hair, cleaning my teeth. When faced with pajama options, I thought fondly back to a time when the preferable choice would be none. Leaking breasts made that a no-go, not to mention the lack of desire to see my body in that way. I did grab a nicer nightshirt rather than flannel pants and a long T-shirt.

It was a step.

Racing to my side of the bed, I slid under the covers, proud of myself for getting done before Aidan got in the room.

My head hit the pillow and I promptly fell asleep.

Chapter 4

Tagging in a Ringer

idan
The coffee maker hissed as the first drops hit the bottom of the empty pot. I pulled down two mugs, wondering if I should get Gracie's ready for her. Mia was still out, proving that miracles did exist, though I assumed we'd hear from her at any moment. She was just starting to stretch out time between the nighttime feedings. We'd hit four hours of sleep around a month and a half, but for the past six weeks, the most we'd managed was four and a half hours. Last night? Five and a half and counting. I'd actually crept into her room this morning to make sure she was fine and had been overjoyed to see her sleeping peacefully.

Now we just needed to pray it was the start of a pattern. Was two nights in a row of this too much to ask for?

A movement by the doors to the backyard caught my eye. Baxter was standing at the door on our deck with a look of disgust because he'd likely been waiting for me for all of a minute. Spoiled pup. However, he was rocking his new sweater. I took another pic for the guys, shooting it off in our group text before letting him in and then quickly putting his food bowl on the floor so he could do his thing with no delay.

As I headed back to the kitchen, I considered our day. Grace had a shift at the library, subbing in for a sick employee during the story hour portion of the morning. I briefly considered bringing Mia. She couldn't sit like the toddlers or anything, but Grace was big on reading stories to her even at three months old. Heck, she'd read stories to her belly all through her pregnancy. I even had from time to time. My favorite had been about a dance in a barnyard. Still loved that one.

After her shift, maybe we could decorate the tree? The Fraser fir we'd gotten from the tree farm outside Champaign had been in a stand in the corner of the family room since the week after Thanksgiving. At first our excuse for putting off decorating was that the branches needed to settle. Now? We simply hadn't found the time.

Last night I'd thought maybe I could get some time with Gracie after she was done with her bath and I got Mia down. I'd wanted to check in with Grace, see if I could get her to open up about what had been clearly upsetting her at the library that morning. However, by the time I got to our room, she was sacked out. The lights were on, but not even that was keeping her up.

I lay there, watching her sleep, and briefly wished for simpler times. The first time we met, at the library in college, I'd helped her. She'd had tears in her eyes, a nose as red as Rudolph from some cold, and couldn't think straight as she tried to write her paper. I talked her down, and that was the end of it—there was never anyone else who caught my eye. Every year we spent together, I grew to love her more. Never had I felt any distance between us. Until now.

I mean, hell, I was missing her even though she was right next to me, but there was *something* I was not seeing, and I hated that she was struggling and I couldn't fix it.

Enough of that. I knew who I needed to talk to. Propping my phone against the backsplash, I hit the button to call my mom before stopping to consider the time. I didn't get a chance to hang up, however, since the FaceTime was accepted almost immediately.

"My darling boy, isn't before seven on a Saturday a tad early even for a morning person such as yourself?" My mom's warm face filled the screen and immediately gave me some reassurance simply by her presence.

"Hey, Mom, had a few minutes before your granddaughter rises for the day and we all fall in line to wait on her—"

"As you should."

"—of course, of course. Thought I'd call real quick and see how you were doing."

My mom was on the move, and I recognized that she'd reached the nook in the corner of her kitchen, which had a table and bench seats. I'd done my homework at that table all through school, talking to her as she danced around the kitchen while cooking. Mom settled in and, assuming not much had changed, propped her phone against the bowl on the table that held apples as she sat back with a coffee mug in her hands. She blew at the top of her coffee while staring at me in the phone, a calculated gaze of hers that I knew well as she seemed to consider what to say.

"Son, out with it. You are practically squirming with the need to say something."

I groaned, dropping my head in my arms. "I think something is wrong with Grace."

"Aidan."

Not sure how my mom translated that mumbled sentence, which had been directed at the table, but clearly she did, because her tone said to sit up and pay attention. I did just that.

"Let's not freak out Mom today. What do you mean, something is wrong with Grace?"

Embarrassment washed over me. I hadn't meant to worry her and hated to stress her out at all. Was this even necessary? Meeting her gaze, I apologized. "Sorry, Mom. I'm probably overreacting. Forget I said anything."

"Try again, son. Spill." She sat back and took a sip of coffee.

Hopefully Grace and Mia were still out. I felt a bit like I was spilling secrets, but I loved Grace too much to ignore her tears the day before.

"Yesterday I stopped by the library, and when I saw Gracie, she'd clearly been crying." My heart was thumping out a nervous beat, but I continued. "I love her so much, Mom, and I feel like I'm missing something here."

Mom sat there, still drinking her coffee, then tilted her head to the side as she considered something. "How much is Mia sleeping at night?"

"Typically four hours, or a touch more. This morning she's exceeded that by an hour, but who knows how long that will last."

Mom nodded. "And Grace is still nursing at night?"

"Yep. She's a rock star."

"And how's your sex life?"

Head to counter again. "Mom." Eye contact was to be avoided here.

"Don't *Mom* me, son. I don't need details, but you know my thoughts on sex—it's a healthy part of any relationship. And I'm guessing by that reaction, it's not happening.

Which, at this point of your baby's life, is pretty natural. Sleep is rare and, when found, not to be squandered. I haven't wanted to insert myself in your lives since I was down there when Mia came home from the hospital, but what if I come down for a few nights and take the nighttime hours to let you both sleep? Or whatever, if you catch my drift. Heck, you could go to an Airbnb in town and I'll stay at your place. I'm open to whatever works for you both."

I considered if Grace would go for that. Maybe? Though I bet she wouldn't want to actually leave yet.

Mom cleared her throat, catching my attention. "One more thing, Aidan."

"Yeah?"

"Your dad and I were married for about eight years before you came along. We were so grateful for you; babies are a gift."

I nodded, waiting for the truth bomb that I could feel coming.

"And it was also the hardest time in our marriage by far."

I shook my head, trying to figure out what in the hell she'd just said. "Why?"

Mom shrugged, taking another drink of her coffee before continuing. "Who knows? I don't know if everyone feels like we did, but we knew how to be a couple. We'd navigated the waters of early marriage easily. We loved spending time together and figured kids would be an easy next step. Spoiler alert—they weren't."

I sat up straight and tried to look indignant. "I have no idea what you are talking about. I was all sunshine and rainbows."

She laughed long and hard, a little too long and hard if you ask me. "Sure, baby. All I'm saying is going from being able to be independent to having to build your entire life around this little being that you love with your whole heart is a bit of a mind switch. An adjustment period is completely normal. Just be there for each other and work on communication."

I thought about it, knowing she was right. "Well, in the spirit of communication, let me talk to Grace about having you come down before just springing it on her."

"Springing what on me?" Grace's voice came from the hall.

I looked over to see the two loves of my life coming into the kitchen. I hadn't even noticed anything on the baby monitor. Grace's hair was tousled and longer than she usually liked. Mia had a crease from sleeping on her face but also an open-mouthed smile. I leaned over to kiss them both, pulling Mia to hold her on my hip.

"Hey, Sophia," Grace called, waving to my mom.

"Morning, my beauties," my mom replied.

I looked at Gracie and decided to just spill. "I told my mom about your tears yesterday—"

"Aidan!" Grace's cheeks heated.

"I know, baby, but I just want to take care of you. You know that. Anyway, Mom said she could come down and do any nighttime feedings for a few nights if we wanted to store up some extra sleep." I mean, I'd also like some other activities to happen, but right then I'd settle for Grace looking rested with no red-rimmed eyes *or* dark circles under them.

"Oh, Sophia, we don't want to put you out." Grace looked to my mom.

"Pshaw, you know what a hardship it would be for me to spend time with my only grandchild. I'd love it with everything in me. You two just need to decide if that's something you both want."

Grace looked to me and bit her bottom lip.

"What do you say, Grace-alicious? Want to hire my mom to babysit for a couple of nights? I mean, both Declan and I survived childhood, so she has a decent track record."

Grace slapped my shoulder while my mom laughed.

"Sorry, Grace, I tried to raise him with more manners."

Grace's laughter was magic to my ears. "You gave it a solid effort, Sophia. And"—she looked to me and shrugged—"if you want to come down for a couple of nights, I think we'd really appreciate it, though I want to stay here and I can't guarantee I won't want to nurse, but you can handle putting her down afterward if that's okay."

Sophia raised her coffee mug to me. "Honey, I'll be there in four hours. I'm off to pack." She ended the call.

Grace met my eyes and winked at me. "So you tagged in a ringer, hmm?"

"Baby"—I pressed a kiss to her forehead—"I will do whatever I need to so that you can rest."

"Thanks." She sank against me for a moment as the three of us stood there, my arms around them both.

All too quickly, she pushed back. "Breakfast?"

"Let me."

Grace's expression turned firm. "No way, mister. You have been doing everything around here. You go sit your happy a—, um, tushy, down and—"

"Tushy?"

"Go with it. I'm trying not to cuss as much. Sit your tushy down and let me make breakfast."

"What are we having?" I asked as I moved to the family room to lay Mia down on the play mat.

"French toast sound good to you? I nursed Mia before

coming down, and I'm famished." She hummed to herself as she started gathering the needed supplies.

I watched the woman I loved more than life move around the kitchen. Some of the glow that she'd been missing for weeks was there even if it was just a sparkle. Maybe she just needed some restful sleep? If so, Mom couldn't get here fast enough. I'd pin Grace to the bed for forty-eight hours straight if it would make her feel like herself again.

Chapter 5

Daycare Dilemmas

Grace

Tim and I were operating like a well-oiled machine. To be fair, the two of us had run more than one story hour completely on our own over the years. Today, however, he was in his element. His T-shirt game was strong, as always. This morning's ensemble was complete with one that was in rainbow print and said TRY READING BOOKS INSTEAD OF BANNING THEM. I mean, in our current climate? So much truth.

Tim finished up story time with a picture book from author Travis Jonker called *Just One Flake*. The kids had a blast creating snowflakes with paper and scissors like the ones visible beneath the cover of the book. Honestly, it was a giant mess, but so worth it for the laughter and joy that permeated the library. Before we knew it, the hour had passed. Our space quickly emptied as I watched more than one happy child tip their heads back to try to catch a snowflake on their tongue as walked into the snow, just like Liam had in the story.

As I relaxed behind the circulation desk and Tim leaned against it and caught his breath, Emma rushed in with coffees in a tray. She'd clearly made a stop at the Sanctuary Café a few blocks away.

She placed the tray on the desk. "So sorry. I tried to get here earlier, but I promised Allyson I'd do the yoga class this morning with her. I didn't want to bail because I feel like I've flaked out a lot lately."

I noted Emma's drawn expression, like she was truly worried about our reaction. "Flaked out or felt like crap for the first trimester and passed on anything that sounded remotely related to exercise?" I asked, shooting her a knowing look. I mean, my first trimester felt as if it was both eons ago and like it was just yesterday.

Tim slid a rolling chair in her direction, and Emma gave him a small smile as she gratefully sank down in it.

"Thanks, Timmy. And I mean, I can't complain. My first trimester was a breeze compared to some of you, but yeah, it kept me from yoga a lot over the past few months."

Tim interrupted the conversation with a hand on one hip and a finger wagging with personality. "One, Timmy? No, just no. And two, not to be rude and act uninterested in this conversation, but is that coffee for me?"

Emma sat up, remembering herself, and began doling out the beverages. "Sorry, Timothy," she said with a smirk.

His expression said no to that too.

Emma soldiered on. "I'm also becoming forgetful. Is pregnancy brain a thing?" She looked at both of us, then waved the words away. "Doesn't matter. Grace, I got you a peppermint mocha decaf."

I took the proffered beverage, inhaling the delicious aroma.

"And Tim, I got you a gingerbread latte."

Tim's smile was wide as he took his drink. "I do love a good gingerbread man. Or a bad one at that. Thanks, girl."

I took a long sip, feeling the deliciousness seep into my bones. After enjoying that sip, I set my coffee to the side and regarded my friend. "This is supersweet, Emma, but you know we have coffee here and your grandma's hot chocolate mix to add in. Why the fancy coffee this morning? I hope you know you didn't owe us anything. You weren't scheduled this weekend, and you know Gabby said she'd come in to cover the afternoon with Tim."

Tim shot me a cross look. "Shush, Grace. I'm happy for coffee from the Sanctuary anytime Emma wants to bring it. Sweetums, I'd be glad to give you a guilt trip if it means more coffee for me. Just say the word."

"Timotheus, hush your mouth." Emma said with a wink that was pretty saucy for her as she raised her beverage in his direction.

"God no. Simply Tim will do just fine."

I choked on my coffee. "Tim, you're anything but simple."

"True that," he said as I got distracted by the ring of my cell phone.

Leaning over, I opened one of the desk drawers where I'd stashed my cell. Usually it sat in my purse upstairs, but I'd wanted Aidan to have zero concern about reaching me if something were to happen to Mia. I knew it was overboard —if anything, Mia was better off with Aidan than me. Or at least it seemed like it when I thought about my beautiful husband, who took everything in stride compared to my new brain that liked to whirl with worry. Still, I'd been concerned I wouldn't hear my phone upstairs and couldn't stomach that thought.

With a glance at my phone, I struggled to make sense of the call. It was Cheryl, our daycare provider once Aidan went back to work next month.

"Sorry, guys, I need to take this," I whispered to Emma and Tim.

Emma made a shooing gesture, and I headed to the kitchen in the back of the library with my phone.

I clicked on the button to accept the call, sinking into the kitchen's couch as I did so. "Hey, Cheryl."

Cheryl sounded breathless. "Grace, I'm so sorry to bother you on the weekend, but I wanted to call you immediately."

My stomach dropped as my ever-helpful brain began immediately catastrophizing, going through all the worst-case scenarios I could think of.

"Are you okay?" I figured I should start with the most pertinent information.

"Yes, aren't you sweet to ask. It's just that we learned last night that Gus was approved for a transfer at work and we're moving to South Carolina. Can you believe it? We'll be closer to our daughter, and the weather, well, what an improvement it will be over Illinois. But I hate leaving you and my families in the lurch. I'm giving everyone a month's notice, though that will be right when you were going to start anyway, but I wanted you to know now so you could make other plans. Again, I'm so sorry..."

Cheryl was still talking, but my brain was racing. Worst-case scenario? Yep, we were there. Highland Falls was many things—heck, many good things. However, the ease with which you could find decent daycare was not what we were known for. No way, no how.

I thought of the possibilities in town that I'd already tried. Maggie and Sully had El going to the newer daycare/preschool called Farm School with Sully's parents, Anna and Lee, as backup. Anna had offered to stay with El, but Maggie and Sully loved the spot they'd found and were happy with their choice.

Emma and Max planned on taking Emma—and Sully's —mom up on her generous offer, however. Their baby would stay with Anna for the first year, then go to daycare.

But grandparents as daycare weren't in the cards for us. My parents were still full-time professors and, honestly, preferred that over parenting. Good people, just very focused on their jobs, and I'd accepted that. They clearly wouldn't be able to pinch-hit for us even if they didn't live in Madison, which was over two hundred miles away. And Aidan's mom still worked part-time. Also, the Farm School'd had zero openings when I checked months ago. Heck, I'd even checked with Ivy's daycare provider, Teri. No spots open there either. Panic began setting in. My stomach churned. My heart raced. And my brain was in overdrive.

"Grace? Grace?"

I started, glancing at the phone in my hand. Oh, Cheryl. "Sorry, Cheryl, I'm here. My mind was just already spinning. But I'm so excited for you all to be closer to your daughter."

"Thanks, sweetheart. Now, if your sweet babe was older, I'd have some great suggestions for you. The daycare on the edge of town that's on an honest-to-goodness farm is delightful, but they have a limited number of infant spots and those are all full. Babies are tough in our little town, but if you're willing to drive to Champaign, you'll have plenty of options."

Champaign. My heart sank. That was an extra sixty miles of driving a day for daycare. It would be different if

Aidan and I were already commuting for work to the larger town, but to drive over there just for daycare… I couldn't imagine doing that.

My breath was coming in shorter bursts, and I needed to get the heck off the phone. Attempting to sound as normal as I could, I got out "Cheryl, thanks so much for giving us a heads-up. Aidan and I wish you all the best in your move and your new home."

"You too, sweetie."

She might have had more to say, but that was all I could handle. I ended the call and dropped my head between my knees. Didn't that help you catch your breath?

What on earth were we going to do now?

The click of someone's shoes reminded me I wasn't alone, though for the life of me, I couldn't care less at the moment.

"Tim, you were right," I heard Emma call from near the door to the kitchen. "Looks like we're in crisis mode."

Within seconds, Emma was by my side on the couch, rubbing my back. "What is it, Gracie?"

I moaned into my lap.

Tim came in and stood in front of me. I knew because his Pride Converses were in my field of vision. "Who do I need to kill or maim?" His toe tapped.

"I can't be a stay-at-home mom," I murmured. "Zero offense meant; I bow down to anyone who can do it. I just know that I will wither and die." I pulled myself to a sitting position, then looked with watery eyes from Emma to Tim, then back. "I didn't shower for a week at a time in Mia's first month."

"Oh, sweetheart, I hope that wasn't a secret. You were looking rough there at the beginning. And, honestly, your hair could still use a trim." Tim's fingers ran through my too-long locks as he doled out his brutal truths.

I worked to ignore his commentary as I dropped my head to Emma's shoulder. Making an appointment for a haircut was a step too far right now. There was zero chance that I could manage that. Heck... maybe I couldn't even afford one anymore.

"Grace, what was the phone call about?" Emma wrapped her arm around me.

"Our daycare provider, Cheryl. She called to say that her husband has accepted a job transfer to South Carolina." I closed my eyes, my brain mentally rearranging my life as I searched for answers that weren't there.

Emma let out a surprised sound as she squeezed my waist. "Oh no. I remember how excited you were when you found her."

Wordlessly I nodded, misery swamping my insides. Tim left and came back quickly with the plate of chocolate chip cookies we'd passed out at the story time. Sugar wouldn't solve this problem, but a delicious cookie was a good try. I took one and so did Emma and Tim as he sat down on my other side so that I was bookended by my two friends. We touched our cookies together before munching in silence.

Finally I spoke up. "I guess I'll just have to find a way to stay home."

To which Tim gasped and Emma said, "Hell no."

I thought of Mia and the lack of options. It made zero rational sense, but I felt rejected, like no one wanted us, which wasn't true, but my brain was telling me it was. And in the middle of that bit of emotion, I could feel my breasts beginning to let down milk because of course they were.

"Grrrr," I growled because apparently that was who I'd

become, a woman who growled. Seemed logical. "I need to pump."

"I'm out." Tim was up and fled the kitchen in record time. He called out to us as he headed back to the front of the library. "I'll just be out here working. You two do whatever you need to do."

Emma gave me a mischievous look. "So apparently we've learned how to get rid of Tim in a hurry. Well done."

She tugged me up and we headed upstairs to my office. After pushing me gently into my chair, she plopped my bag in front of me as she closed the door and took her own seat in the armchair she favored. "No modesty today—like I said, *crisis mode*. Feel free to toss a blanket over yourself if you'd like, but I've seen Maggie pump more than I can count. Now what's this about staying home? I know you love your little peanut, but that's always something you've said wouldn't make you happy."

Once I was all hooked up, I looked over to Emma. "You don't need to avert your eyes; I brought my wearable pumps today." I gestured at my nursing bra, which still covered me while pumping, and Emma's eyes widened.

"Maggie didn't have that," she said.

"Pros and cons of this one, but it does make it easier to have a conversation." I gave her a sad smile as I thought of my problem, which had no solution I could see. Taking a big breath, I tried to summarize what was whirling in my mind. "First, I should absolutely acknowledge that this is a first-world problem. My baby is healthy. My husband is wonderful—"

"Other than the not-jumping-your-bones thing."

"Now you sound like our middle school book club, but yeah, that's still an issue. But this new one is moving to the forefront. Finding great daycare stressed me out when we got pregnant. You know we checked everywhere. Cheryl only had an opening because she had a family move. Now I'm back to square one, *and* all the other families at her place will be looking too." I rested my head on my hand, wishing for a simple answer that I knew didn't exist.

"And you think the best choice is leaving your job here?" Emma asked, skepticism evident.

At her words, the door to the office opened. I looked down and realized my nursing bra covered the most important spots, but I was still ready to have words with whoever had walked in here when I saw it was Maggie.

She held up her hands. "Sorry. Tim told me you were pumping, but he also sent me a SOS text, and I was just down the street at the café with Sully, so I rushed over. What gives?"

"Grace is thinking of giving up her job." Emma's voice had lost any sparkle, and I felt the same.

"What?" Maggie screeched.

We quickly filled her in, talking over each other as we unloaded. Finally I looked from Emma to Maggie and shrugged. "I just don't see another choice. You know I called everywhere in town months ago. I need to run the numbers to even see if we can afford to drop down to one salary. I mean, it would be tight, but likely doable. I just wish there was another answer."

I dropped my head to my desk, misery washing over me.

Maggie put a hand on my head. "Babe, we're going to help you figure this out. Now finish up this pumping and we can head to the brewery if you like. Tim said Gabby will be here soon with that crazy cat, Aslan. He said you two didn't need to stay, they had it. And"—she paused until I sat up and looked her way—"you need to fill me in on this whole hands-free pumping situation you've got going on here. How did I miss out on this for the past year?"

I gave Maggie a tearful smile as I squeezed her hand, grateful that she was trying to lighten the conversation. She was right—we'd figure something out. We had to.

Chapter 6

Middle of the Morning

***A**idan*

Levi ran up the snowy streets ahead of me as I fought to find a deeper well of energy to get another burst of speed from my tired legs. Turning at the city pool, we headed back down a small hill and started toward downtown while the sky became a snow globe.

My speed increased as our legs stretched out toward the end of our five-mile run. Our route took us across the state road, which was getting slick with accumulating snowfall, and then we headed up the small hill toward the business district and the streets around the old courthouse at the center of town. Levi reached the low wall that marked the lawn that surrounded the building first, sitting down as he watched me slide to a stop in front of him.

"You're getting faster," I said, dropping my hands to my knees as I fought to catch my breath.

"Nah, you're just getting old, pops," Levi replied with a smirk, his own hands resting on top of his head as his breathing began to return to normal.

Levi had moved to Highland back in the spring. His

twin brother, Logan, was already here, had been for several years. Their parents were recent residents as well. Levi worked remotely doing digital editing, so his flexible schedule made him an ideal running partner as my shifts were sometimes irregular with my occasional overnights, depending on the schedule. He ran with Logan quite a bit too, and I sometimes joined them, but we got out at least two times a week to run through town instead of the trails at the park.

I dropped next to him on the wall, looking at the white lights around the square. They were lit up even at lunchtime, but the gray day benefited from them. The warm glow gave the entire space a feeling like I'd walked into one of the Hallmark holiday movies Mom loved to have on the television this time of year.

"This is some Christmas-card shit," Levi said, gesturing around us.

"That it is."

I felt Levi look my way. "You want to tell me why you started today's run like you were being chased? There's a reason you were dragging ass at the end, you know."

I hung my head. He was right, and the churning in my gut hadn't lessened during the last five miles.

"You not loving being dad on duty?"

My head spun to Levi. "Hell, no. Hanging out with Mia is the best." We sat in silence for a beat before I continued. "I just feel like I'm failing Grace."

Levi gave a murmur of understanding before he stood and kicked my leg. "Let's do our cool-down jog to your place for this conversation. It's a bit chilly for sitting on the stone wall here—my ass is numb."

I chuckled, hauling myself up, and we started our slow jog toward home.

He gave me a block before calling me out. "So how are you failing your girl? Thought you two were solid."

"Thought so too. I mean, we are for the most part. It's just... we've been together for years, since we were kids in college. But now? Since Mia was born, there's been this distance."

We turned down Main Street, careful of our steps. This part of town had the original brick-lined street that ran a few blocks. Cool, sure, but a bitch to run on.

"What are you going to do about it?" Levi asked as we quickly took another right back to a normal road as we finished the last few blocks of our run.

"Well, I called in reinforcements." I gestured to the car in my driveway up ahead. "My mom."

Levi hooted. "You called your mom?"

"Tell me you wouldn't pull Linnie in if you were desperate to help some girl you loved." I gave him a skeptical look. Liam and Logan's mom, Linnie, lived for helping out her boys.

"I'm not going to have to worry about that for some time. I'm off relationships." Levi shook his head.

"Really? Even with curvy blondes that love nothing more than to argue with you?"

Levi's sister-in-law was Allyson. Allyson's sister, Maeve, was in and out of Highland Falls as she flitted about the Midwest—hell, the country. Anytime I saw her with Levi, the sparks flew. The question was whether there was romantic attraction or just a desire to piss each other off. Jury was still out on that one.

"Not going there for a variety of reasons, man."

"But no denial that you'd like to? Hmm, interesting."

"Back to the tag in of your mom." Levi pointed at my mom's Subaru Outback in the drive.

I shrugged. "Called her this morning and unloaded. She pointed out that Grace and I are sleep-deprived. Offered to come down and take nighttime duty for a few. Grace readily agreed. Mom got here an hour or so ago, and Grace is working at the library this morning—" The vibration from my phone stopped my conversation as I pulled it out to see if Grace needed anything.

"All good?" Levi asked.

I choked out a laugh after reading the message. "It's from Emma. She says Grace wants me to come to the Homestead, but she's had two beers, so she's not sure how long she'll be awake."

"One, thought she was at work."

I shrugged, shooting a text back to Emma. "I'm guessing they got done and headed that way."

"And two"—Levi glanced at the time on his Garmin—"two beers by one p.m. on a Saturday. Your girl is starting early."

I shrugged. "She hasn't really drunk much of anything since before Mia was conceived. Maybe she needs to unwind." I started walking up my drive backward, finishing our conversation but also wanting to get to Gracie. "Whatever it is, I know I want to see it. Feel like a burger?"

Levi headed over to his 4Runner. "I've gotta head home to shower and check on a few things. If I can, I'll swing by."

I waved in his direction and turned to jog inside. Now to let my mom know she was on solo duty for a while longer. She would not consider that a hardship.

* * *

The Homestead wasn't rocking out on a Saturday afternoon, which wasn't shocking. The majority of the lunch crowd had come and gone. The railroad museum in town did some train rides all through December on the weekends, allowing kids to have lunch with Santa. That did increase the amount of out-of-towners throughout the month, which some of us townies grumped at—good-naturedly of course.

Judging by the people gathered at some of the tables around the brewery, Santa visits via the train had already happened for several families. However, the parents likely wanted more food than the complimentary PB&J sandwich that came with every train ride, no matter how delicious they might be. Thus, the families dotting the dining room of the brewery. Everywhere you looked, kids were coloring holiday papers at the tables as the parents had a beverage and sat in peace under the evergreen-swagged walls of the brewery, the requisite mistletoe, lights, and Christmas trees placed throughout the dining area.

The coloring pages were a new addition here, one of many. Once Sully became a dad with the arrival of El, and Jake by marrying Ivy and getting the bonus of Addie, the two of them looked at the "pleasures" of dining out with kids a little differently. As a result, there were now a variety of toys to entertain kids available for checkout at the hostess station in the brewery. New coloring pages that were changed weekly were also available, and completed masterpieces were hung up on the bulletin board by the front door. There was also a new chalk wall on one side of the dining room where kids could create some artwork as their parents decompressed. Laurie said it had brought in more young families because they felt welcomed instead of being considered a nuisance.

While the kids hard at work on their pages were adorable, the woman I was looking for was sitting in the bar area. She was at a low table with a couch and an armchair and two forms of trouble in the way of Emma and Maggie sitting on either side. Their eyes tracked me as Grace had her head resting against the couch, eyes closed, singing "Middle of the Morning" by one of her favorite artists, Jason Isbell and the 400 Unit.

Maggie went to tap her, and I held up a hand to hold her off. Gracie was clearly feeling good, but I knew this woman. She wasn't drunk. Without missing a beat, she sang along word for word as the song flowed from the speakers in the brewery.

As she belted out the lyrics about being tired, she held her arms up, pouring out her feelings to the room without even a glance to see who was listening. Emotions filled the space. At first I smiled. But then I saw a tear sneak out from below her closed lids.

Shit.

I moved without the conscious decision to do so. Emma hopped up, and I quickly stole her seat to sit down next to Grace. She felt the movement, and her eyes shot open and she looked from Emma, now standing, to me.

"Hey, Grace-alicious, what are these tears about?" I whispered, wiping away the one that was dancing on her lower lids.

More appeared as she slid into my arms and tucked her head into my neck. While I was worried, I also had to admit that holding her felt so good. It had been so long.

"Babe, what's going on?" I nodded as Maggie caught my eye and pointed to the bar. She got up and joined Emma at the stools, still watching me. I knew they were aware I had Grace, but I also knew they'd go to bat for their friend, no matter how long we'd been married, if they felt like I was being a fool. Damn, I was grateful she had friends like those two.

"Cheryl called me when I was at the library." Her lips moved against my neck.

I could feel the tension in her body as she spoke. It took me a second to remember who the hell Cheryl even was, but then it came to me. Daycare. No idea why she'd need to call now though. We weren't starting until mid-January.

"What did she need?" I spoke into her hair because she was still hugging me like some kind of koala. I ran a hand down her back, hoping it was remotely soothing as I took a deep breath, then another. It worked, and I felt Grace match my breathing as a little tension left her.

"She's moving." While she was more relaxed, I could feel that she was teetering on the edge of some big emotions. "And you know I called around before we found her. I'm just... I just... It's just... I don't know what to do, Aidan. I love my job. And I love Mia, I really do. But when I was home with her, it was like I lost, I don't know, I lost *me*."

Grace pulled back and looked at me, tears now free-falling. Her hands flailed as she gestured toward a speaker. "It's like Isbell says in that song—I finally felt the light come in *this week* when I went back to work. I hadn't realized how much I'd lost until I found it again. I'd somehow lost myself. I loved being with Mia, but I can't find the balance at home. I don't know what's wrong with me."

"Shhhh." I pulled her close, squeezing her tight. Damn, I wish she'd told me some of this when she'd been home for the past three months. "Babe, I totally understand. You do a fabulous job at the library, and I know how much you love it. Why do you think that needs to change?"

Grace sat up and raised her arms in a movement of frustration. "Well, what else are we going to *do*, Aidan? I can't bring her to the library with me, and she clearly can't go to the jail with you, so I guess I'm staying home."

I shook my head in confusion. "Grace, no. This doesn't automatically fall to you. I don't know what the answer is yet, but it isn't you staying home. No. You are an amazing mother, but that isn't what you want, so we're going to figure something out."

She fell against me, dropping her head to my shoulder. "You don't think I'm terrible because I don't want to be home full-time?"

I put my hand on her head, holding her as close as I could. "Of course not. You are amazing with Mia. We will find another answer."

"Promise?"

"Promise," I whispered as my mind started racing for how we were going to fix this one.

Chapter 7

Glitter in the Air

Grace

My red wrap dress swished around my knees as I moved around the tables in the library and admired the setup for the holiday decorations that some of our young library patrons were creating to take home that afternoon. The Christmas trees were next level, and I loved it anytime the library was filled with the artwork of the children who visited.

"Grace." Gabby waved to me from the circulation desk, so I headed in her direction.

"Yeah, Gabs?" I asked, running a hand down the back of Gabby's cat, Aslan, who was swishing her tail as she strutted over the table with a very vocal greeting.

"Ben's mom was by earlier. She wanted to thank you for the Hanukkah focus in the library at the start of December."

"Not necessary," I said, my brain running through a mental list of the things we needed to do still for our open house this afternoon.

"I told her you'd say that. She wanted me to remind you that as a member of one of the only Jewish families in town, she's very grateful that both our library and schools have been so inclusive without even having to be asked."

"I'm glad they feel welcome, but it seems like the least we could do," I pointed out. We highlighted books written by Jewish authors, had a few dreidel art projects, sang some songs during story time. Bare minimum, and I strived to do more in the future. But we worked to be inclusive of all holidays, so of course we weren't going to leave Hanukkah out.

Gabby shrugged and then picked up Aslan off the table to plop her down on the floor. "At any rate, how can I help, boss? Anything you need to get ready?"

I ran over what we had left for our afternoon celebration, giving Tim and Emma jobs as they appeared. Our volunteer Santa Claus, Scott, was set up in the children's-book room near the fireplace in an armchair, ready for pictures with kids. We had a sugar-cookie decorating station in the kitchen. Art stations were scattered among the tables in the fiction and nonfiction rooms. And story hour with some holiday books would be going on for the entire two hours—we were each taking shifts—in the foyer with the reader on the grand staircase and the kids gathered below on the floor in front of the circulation desk. Spiced cider was available for all, and we hoped parents would sit back and relax. It was such a busy season—we wanted to give them this moment of calm before the storm.

Three hours later, the four of us were collapsed in various states around the kitchen. Tim had glitter in his hair, which honestly wasn't all that surprising. Gabby had paint on her shirt. Emma was wearing antlers on her head, but she might have had those on when she arrived. And my dress had held up, but I felt like a Mack truck had run me over at some point in the evening.

Tim spoke up from his prone location on the couch.

"Please remind me to tell Eric that our cat and two pups are enough. Children are adorable, but that's how they trick you, and the next thing you know, they've suckered you into a glitter art project when we all know glitter was created by Satan."

"Here, here." Gabby raised her arm in exhausted solidarity. "Aslan is it for me."

Emma rubbed her belly with a sheepish expression. "It's too late for me and Grace over here."

"Suckers," Tim muttered.

"True that," Gabby said, reaching out to kick my foot to lighten the statement.

Tim shot me a look. One, I will note, that was really *not* filled with remorse. "How pissed are you about the glitter, boss? I mean, in my defense, I thought it would be a sprinkle here and there, not full-blown *glitter in the air*."

"Should we call you Pink?" Gabby asked with a raised brow.

"The woman is a beast. I'd love to be compared to her," Tim said. "But as I was saying, the kid had a great argument about said glitter making the snow come alive in his painting. Who the hell knew kids couldn't sprinkle?"

Gabby spoke up, frighteningly matching my thoughts. "Everyone, Tim. *Everyone* knows kids make messes with glitter."

"I'm sure we'll get it all cleaned up," he shot back.

"Not a chance." Gabby shook her head at him. "We're going to be finding glitter throughout this place until we all retire. Mark my words."

"And you think you could leave this?" Emma gestured toward Gabby and Tim.

I immediately groaned. When Cheryl called the other day, Tim had known I'd been upset and that I had mentioned staying home, but he thought that conversation had been dropped. I hadn't shared that I'd actually considered, albeit briefly, staying home because, well, everyone would know why in three... two... one...

"I'm sorry, *what?*" The *what* was screeched. I mean, it's the only way to describe it.

"Calm down, Tim—" I started, hands up in a calming gesture.

"Don't try to calm me down, missy. What does Emma mean, 'leave this'? I thought that had been settled?"

I sighed. Never let it be said that Tim didn't have feelings. Big feelings. I mean, on the positive side, it also meant I knew we all mattered to him a heck of a lot. It also meant that I loved his partner, Eric, for many things—including the fact that he kept Tim on an even keel.

"The woman I'd found for in-home daycare for Mia called yesterday. She's moving to South Carolina—"

Tim interrupted because he is the most impatient man on earth. "I know that, Grace, but I thought we covered what a hot mess you were for the past three months." His arms flailed like a Muppet. "No, Grace, just no. I'm so sorry. I know what a headache it was to find even that place." Tim popped up from the couch and began pacing around the kitchen, circling the farm table in the middle, as his hands continued to fly about while he talked. "Okay, this is fine, we're fine. Between the four of us, we know the whole town. Who can we call? There's got to be something." He came to a stop in front of me and leaned against the counter, hand on his hip, finger wagging in my face. "Because if you think you're leaving this place, you have another thing coming. You *are* the Ryan Library. I mean, we're no slouches"—he gestured back at Gabby and Emma—"and the rest of our crew, but you are the one that keeps this place going. You write the grants, do the paperwork that none of us knows how to do—"

"Or wants to do," Emma piped up.

"Amen, sister." Gabby leaned over and high-fived Emma.

"Point being, Grace Russo, we need you and we can't lose you." Tim stood with his hands on his hips, daring anyone to contradict him.

I laughed. I mean, the situation wasn't funny, but it was nice to know I was appreciated, not that I doubted it. "I've got you, Tim. And yes, when Cheryl first called, you saw the tears. They took me to the brewery, and as I mulled it all over, the only solution I saw was my staying home."

Tim started to interrupt me, so I gave him back his own attitude and put up my hand.

"Hold your horses, friend. As I was saying, the only solution I saw then was staying home. Then Aidan met Maggie, Emma, and me at the Homestead. He told me we'd figure it out. When we got home, Sophia was watching Mia, and we shared the new dilemma with her—"

"Sorry—Sophia?" Gabby asked.

"Aidan's mom." I sighed, remembering the conversation over a charcuterie tray Sophia had whipped together the previous afternoon *while* she also managed to watch Mia, do some tummy time, then give her a bath and put her down for a nap. She'd shaken her head at my shocked expression and told me not to compare a veteran to a newbie. I knew she was right, but still. "She agreed that my staying home wasn't the answer, and honestly, she made the choice to have a job while being a mom for similar reasons." That had made me feel better. Admittedly, she wouldn't have been able to stay home once Aidan's dad passed, but before that, she'd chosen to work.

Somehow she'd known I needed to hear that and made sure to share.

"So did you and hubby burn up the sheets last night with a babysitter at your beck and call?" Tim raised his brows, unknowingly hitting on another sore topic.

My face heated as the truth tumbled out. "I fell asleep at seven after we finally decorated our tree and had dinner." I looked down at the floor, tracing the wooden planks with the toe of one of my brown boots.

Emma came to lean against the counter next to me and squeezed my arm. "Sounds like you needed the sleep."

"I did."

"Okay, chickie, listen up." It was hard to take Tim seriously considering his face was positively sparkling in the light of the kitchen. "You're going to march your gorgeous ass home to the hunk of man you have, and then you're going to take advantage of the fact that you don't have to get up with a baby tonight and you'll burn up the sheets, do you hear me? I don't see you on the schedule tomorrow, so I better not see you here. Stay home, soak in all that family time, and come back raring to write some grants or whatever you do up there." He gestured to the ceiling. "Meanwhile, we will be blowing up our phones, checking in on any and all available options for daycare that do not involve you doing something you don't want to do, even for that adorable peanut of yours. You hear me?"

I leaned forward, pressing a kiss to Tim's cheek. I was blessed when it came to my friends. "I hear you Tim."

With goodbyes to Emma and Gabby, I headed out the door and toward home.

It wasn't quite dusk yet, but the air was still. Our small town was typically quiet, but on a Sunday, it was even more so. I took the walk home to try to get my mindset switched.

Tim was right. Sophia was here for the night. Maybe I needed to try to seduce my husband.

Just the thought made me anxious. What if I leaked? What would he think about my belly? Aidan was gorgeous. I mean, the man had been attractive in college and had only grown more handsome as he'd aged. I felt frumpy by comparison. It wasn't like I felt that way because of any snide comments he'd made but because of what I saw when I looked in the mirror. I'd been prepared for pregnancy to change my body—that was expected. What I hadn't planned for was the fact that twelve weeks after Mia's birth, I was still far from what I'd looked like pre-Mia. And, quite frankly, I wasn't sure I would ever look like that again.

That messed with my mind and pissed me off. Never before in my life had I dealt with such insecurity around my body. When I caught a glimpse of myself in the mirror, I struggled to match what I saw with the body I knew. It shook me.

But screw it. Tonight I was going to try to get something started. Maybe if I showed Aidan I was interested, he'd show me the same? What if he was waiting for me to make the first move? He never had before, but I needed to stop assuming the worst here.

As I made the way up the sidewalk to our home, the front door opened and what I saw melted my heart and made me laugh out loud.

"What am I looking at?" I asked as Sophia stepped quickly past me and moved down the steps. Aidan was there with little Miss Mia in the new sling from his coworkers. She had on her adorable Santa hat as she grinned at me, waving her little fist as she opened and closed it. And last but not least, Baxter was wearing the sling-matching pink sweater with trees. I joined my little family and looked up to Aidan.

"What's going on?" I whispered, leaning forward to press a kiss on Mia's little head as she cooed at me, putting her tiny hand on my face.

"Mom and I were talking," Aidan said as he nodded to his mom, now standing on the sidewalk behind us. "We figured she could snap a quick family photo before you came in. I remembered you wore your red dress to work, so we thought it would look festive."

I glanced down at my dress peeking out from the bottom of my thick black jacket, then looked back to his warm brown eyes. "You remembered my dress from this morning?"

Aidan shook his head with a smile. "Of course I did, babe. I don't know if you've really seen yourself in that dress, but I sure have and it's one of my favorites."

My face heated. That was good, right? Maybe he'd been sending me messages that he was still attracted to me and I just hadn't noticed?

Apparently Aidan clocked the expression on my face, because he brought his hand under my chin until I met his eyes again. "Gracie? You okay?"

My eyes watered immediately because I was the person who could no longer control emotions. "Ignore me—I love this idea. Let me just toss my coat inside the front door." Within seconds, I'd moved a step away from him to get rid of said jacket and try to school my emotions before coming back to stand by his side.

"See? Stunning."

I glanced up at Aidan to see him looking at me with an expression I hadn't seen for months. Heated was the only way to describe it.

"Aidan, stop—your mom is here," I murmured, gesturing toward Sophia, who was figuring out how to get her camera app open.

He took a step toward me, sliding a hand behind my back. "Sweetheart, I'm going to need you to hear me when I tell you you're stunning, because I'm just realizing by the look in your eyes that you might not believe me."

I looked away, but he gently turned me back to him. "I'm serious, Grace-alicious, when are you going to realize that I went from being wrapped up in you to wrapped up in us? This little family of ours? I'm all in. There is nowhere I'd rather be."

Yep, I was going to cry and there would be no point in the pictures if I looked like a member of the band KISS. Instead of being a mature adult and responding to his words, I switched topics.

"We need to hurry; Mia doesn't have any socks on," I pointed out.

Aidan ducked until his lips were at my ear. "I'll let you get away with that subject change now, sweetheart, but we will be talking later." He pressed a kiss to my neck before continuing. "And no worries on her precious little toes because, fair warning, my mom has jacked up the heat inside, so we are practically living on a tropical island in there."

"Got it, kids," Sophia called, bringing me back to the present. "Ready?"

I turned my head toward Sophia while I felt Aidan move so that he was kissing my temple, and Mia looked at the camera and I could feel her happy coo as she posed like the model she was.

Wrapped up in us... I guess I could lean into that even if it was romance-book-level schmoopy. But we were going to talk more later? Would that mean just talking or something more? Heck, which did I even want?

Aidan's hand slid lower, landing on my butt as he gave it a squeeze. I felt a flutter of excitement that had lain dormant for too long. Mmmm. Well, I guess that answered that. Oh boy.

Chapter 8

Nothing Compares

Aidan

There was the normal flurry of activity around the "witching hour," as Grace liked to call it. From about four in the afternoon until around seven in the evening, it was all hands on deck. Whether it was my coming home from work in the first weeks to months of Mia's life or now, when it was Grace arriving, this was the time when dinner got prepped, some quick playtime happened, and then we ate, Mia got bathed, and bedtime routines began. In other words, mass chaos, and Mia was often fussy for it, especially in the beginning.

Tonight was even more so. After pictures on the porch, Mia had been grumpier than usual. Nothing seemed to make her happy other than being held. After a few minutes, Grace had noticed Mia's cheeks were rosy and Mom had noticed the soaked bib. Sure enough, Grace checked out her gums and our little peanut had a tooth working on coming in soon. I thought three months might be early, but Mom assured us that both Declan and I had our first tooth around now. Tylenol before bed and nursing should help her relax.

Which simply meant that Grace, as always, had more to do than me or even my mom because when Grace was home, she wanted to nurse and not pump. Even now, after working a full day, she'd need to feed Mia—especially when our little girl was out of sorts.

I got it, I truly did. Mia had lost weight because she'd been born before Grace's milk really came in, and that had stressed Grace out... big time. Mia had been a little jaundiced as well, and I felt like Grace had taken far too much responsibility for getting little Mia back on track. The nurses assured us that she'd be fine, and she had been. But on the journey to Mia being "fine," I could see that Grace was blaming herself for anything that was wrong with our baby, and I hadn't been able to do anything about it.

After it was said and done, the only thing I'd been able to do was support my wife and reassure her that all was well. A result, Grace was adamant that she needed to stick to her nursing schedule even now. I loved that she enjoyed it—nursing was truly a special bond between Grace and Mia—but sometimes I wondered if it was taking too much from her. I mean, she'd already had to carry our baby for forty weeks and deal with all the impact on her body from that, but now she couldn't even go through a five-hour stretch without pumping, even if she wasn't with Mia.

I'd known it wasn't like our lives would go back to "normal" after Mia's birth. We now had a "new normal," as much as I hated that term. Still, I felt like the changes to Grace's day-to-day life seemed far more than mine. It made me bow down to women everywhere. I had no idea how they did it.

Grace had scooped up Mia after the bath and headed to our room to nurse her, saying she'd give her some Tylenol once she was done. I finished wiping down the counters and was going to head up to read Mia a story and get her to bed if she didn't fall asleep nursing. And then Mom was going to give us one last night of babysitting duty before heading home. Admittedly, I was hoping for some time to connect with Grace, but knowing Mia was feeling off, I'd also settle for Grace feeling as well rested as possible.

"Aidan."

I looked over to the couch where my mom sat scrolling on her phone.

She continued without looking up. "I'm sending the pictures I took of you all on the front steps."

The noise from my phone on the counter told me she'd done just that. I picked up my phone to take a look at the pictures she'd sent. Grace was gorgeous, naturally. Mia and Baxter were adorable, especially in their matching sling and dog sweater. I couldn't wait to show the guys.

"Son." My mom's voice was gentle, which made me brace just a bit. What was she about to unload on me? "If you look at the pictures you have on your phone since Mia was born, who's in them?"

I was certain my face showed my confusion at her comment, because she immediately clarified.

"Mia, of course," she prompted. "Is Baxter in them?"

I nodded, thinking of the hundreds, low estimate, of the pictures starring our pup and beautiful baby.

Mom continued, "I'm certain I'm in some from the times I've visited because Grace has sent me those pics. Grace's parents?"

"They came down for an afternoon when Mia was born, so I know she took some of them then."

"You, of course."

I struggled to figure out what she was getting at. Of course there were pictures of me with Mia.

"Yeah, Mom. What are you getting at?"

"Aidan, how many pictures are there of Grace with Mia?"

I started to protest—there were tons of pictures of Grace with Mia. But then I stopped and opened my camera roll. There were the pictures I'd taken of Mia. Some of Mia with Baxter. Lots of me with Mia that Grace had sent me. A few selfies I'd taken with Mia when I had her in a sling. The only one of Mia and Grace together came shortly after she was born. That was it.

I scrolled and scrolled, going over the same pictures a multitude of times. The facts in front of my face didn't matter because this seemed inconceivable, to quote *The Princess Bride*. Looking up at my mom, I knew I was missing something bigger than the lack of pictures of Grace, but what?

"I don't know why I don't have pictures of Grace with Mia."

Mom laid a hand on mine as she quietly asked, "Have you taken any?"

I blinked, looking back at the camera roll. Grace had taken some of me and Mia—why hadn't I done the same? "Is it an excuse if I say I don't think she asked me to?"

Mom looked at my phone with me and pointed to a few pictures. "Did you ask her to take those?"

I shook my head, but she already knew the answer.

"Sweetheart, I can't speak for Grace; I can only speak for myself. And I know there are two parents here, but this seems to be an issue prevalent for moms. Not saying it doesn't happen to dads too. Sometimes, when we become a mom, it's like our former identity ceases to exist. Like our entire worth is tied up in this one role and we lose ourselves a bit in the process. I'm not saying that's happening for

Grace, but you mentioned feeling the distance between you two when you called yesterday. Maybe she's a little lost?"

I gave some thought to her words. They matched some of what Grace had said the other day. "But Mom, what does that have to do with the photos?"

Mom pulled up the picture she'd taken of our family just a few hours before. "I just wonder if in losing herself a little bit, which as I said is totally normal, Grace doesn't see that she's still beautiful and worthy of being in the pictures. She needs to know that you *see* her, Aidan. That you see her as who she was before and who she is now. That you are still attracted to who she has become."

"Of course I'm still attracted to her," I sputtered.

Mom's voice was gentle when she spoke. "Does she know that?"

I thought about Grace's reaction when I said I'd noticed her dress. *Did* she know that? I wanted to say yes, of course, but maybe not? "Mom, am I just a terrible husband?" I slumped down, resting my head in my hands. "I feel like I should know all this. I mean, how do I not know this? Before Mia, Grace and I were solid. How do people do this?"

Mom rubbed my back. "I can't speak for the world, but I mentioned that your dad and I struggled too when you came along. And again when Declan came, though not as much. Your dad said it was like renegotiating the terms of our relationship because conditions had changed. Honestly, I think that's smart. You two got together when you were young, just like we did. *Of course* you will change as you get older. That isn't a problem unless you don't communicate. I think all couples have a choice. They can grow together, or they can grow apart. How you end up is up to you."

I spoke to the counter. "So you're saying I need to talk to her."

She gave me a firm pat on the back. "Yep, and there's no time like the present. I'll hang out here and watch Baxter."

I looked to the corgi, who was crashed out under the Christmas tree in the corner. "Tough job, Mom."

"I know. I might need a glass of beer from that brewery you're all crazy about to tide me over."

"Don't work too hard," I muttered as I headed for our bedroom to the familiar sound of my mom's low laughter.

"It's a hardship, my baby boy."

I shook my head as I listened to Mom talking to Baxter, telling him he was the "goodest dog ever," and I turned the corner into our bedroom. Grace was sitting against the tall wooden headboard, legs stretched out, in multicolored pajama pants and a light blue tank that was pulled up as she nursed Mia, who seemed much more content than she'd been earlier.

Grace didn't even seem to register that I was in the room. Her eyes were closed, her head lightly swaying as she listened to some music coming out of the speaker in the room. I paused, catching the song quickly. It was one of her favorites, Chris Cornell's tribute to Prince with "Nothing Compares 2 U."

I leaned against the wall and watched her, my toes digging into our rug, caught in the beauty of this woman I'd loved for almost a third of my life. There wasn't anything that compared to her. She was my north star.

Grace was lost in the music as she whispered some of the words, clearly trying to stay quiet for little Miss Mia. I shook my head; my girl certainly did love music. Always had.

Actually, come to think of it, Grace hadn't been playing

music since we had Mia. I mean, she had some new kids' music she played occasionally, but it used to be if she was home before me, music would be blaring as she danced around the kitchen, whipping up some dinner as she sang. My gut sank as I realized that had been another change in her that I'd just... missed. Was that due to postpartum depression and I hadn't caught it? Or just a change in what she liked? Seemed like something I should have noticed.

"Are you just going to stand there like a creeper?" Grace's hushed voice brought my attention back to the room.

I looked her way and gave her a sheepish smile. "You caught me. Came up to take the little one to bed and saw you doing your own silent karaoke. Reminded me that I hadn't heard you playing music much lately and wondered why."

Grace shrugged as she looked down to Mia, smoothing a finger across her cheek. "I don't know. Sometimes I feel like blaring music in the kitchen that isn't kids' music might not be good for her." She looked up to him. "Maybe she needs to listen to stuff that's educational or made for kids her age?"

"Gracie," I murmured, crossing the room and catching the lavender scent coming from the diffuser. "All music has value. You can play what you love for Mia. She'll associate that with you."

I considered what she'd said, then thought about her reaction to Mia losing weight when she was first born and the jaundice issue. I thought about what my mom said about Grace not being in pictures—which, frankly, was also on me. We had so much to unpack here, and that didn't even touch the lack of sex or the current daycare crisis we had going on. But I guess I needed to start somewhere. And I had an inkling that dealing with one of the issues Grace was facing would lead to unraveling the others.

"Babe, do you feel like you're a good mom?"

Grace's eyes welling up as she looked at me almost broke my heart. I quickly climbed onto our bed to sit hip to hip, wrapping an arm across her shoulders.

She leaned her head against me, and I almost missed her quiet response. "Sometimes."

"When?"

She ran her hand over Mia's fuzzy little head. Her hair was dark, taking after me, but she certainly didn't have a ton yet. "Times like now."

"So nursing." I glanced at Mia. "She seems to be feeling more like herself."

"For now." Her head bobbed against my chest. "I was so scared when she lost weight when she was born. I know it wasn't a tremendous amount, but when you only weigh seven pounds, every ounce counts."

I made a noise of agreement to keep her talking.

"I got so focused on figuring nursing out. I figured that was something I could do; *I* could give her the tools to stay healthy and nourished."

I pressed a kiss to the top of her head, then smoothed down Mia's foot, which she was poking in my direction as she nursed. My little Rockette doing leg kicks in her footed sleeper that had gingerbread men all over. Adorable, of course.

"I get it, Grace. Parenting is hard, and it is comforting to grab on to what you can actually fix."

She gave a short laugh. "Parenting isn't hard for you."

I froze, thinking about what that might mean to her. Pulling back, I gazed at Grace, who was now looking away from me to focus on Mia. I gently moved her chin to meet my eyes. "Grace, this isn't easy for me."

Her eyes welled up. "But you're so good at it."

I gave her a small smile. "I'm glad you think so. I did help Mom with Declan sometimes, even when I was little, but I'm flying blind here too."

Her cheeks grew rosy, but she kept locked on my gaze, though her voice was so quiet I had to duck down to hear her. Grace was typically confident and assertive. I should have noticed the change in her behavior in the past weeks. But then again, she typically felt like she was in complete control in all situations. I could see how she'd been thrown for a loop here; I was just pissed I'd missed it.

"Sometimes I'm jealous of you."

"Why?"

She appeared uncertain but kept going. "I'm not sure. Like the other day when you took Mia to the Homestead after stopping by the library. You weren't nervous at all. When I took her out by myself when I was on maternity leave, I always worried she might start getting fussy when we were out or something."

I reached over and squeezed her knee. "Thanks for telling me, Gracie." I paused, wanting to make sure she knew I heard her. "When I take Mia out, I feel like if she gets fussy, people should expect that because she's a baby. Do you think people are judging you if she's loud when you're out?" I waited a beat, considering what I'd said, before adding, "It's absolutely okay if you do feel that way or if you don't. Just curious."

"Um, I think so?" She bit her bottom lip.

I thought about that. "Do you think that's part of the unfair pressure we, as a society, put on moms?"

I thought that would get her fired up, and boy was I

right. It was like going back in time to undergrad when she would get on a roll talking about how women were being treated unfairly in terms of pay, access to healthcare, et cetera. Grace often told me that she felt like she came alive in college, that she was inspired to see the world for what it was. Hell, one of the reasons she got a master's in library science was that she saw the public library as a great equalizer in our society. It was nice to see her fire come back, even if it was a dull roar.

Grace sat up, nodding to herself as she did a quick switch of sides with a burp for Mia in between. "Oh my gosh—you're right." She groaned. "What is wrong with me? I mean, why am I falling for this BS in our society that a mom has to be superwoman and a guy is amazing if he just spends time with his kid every once in a while?" She rested her head on the bed, looking to the ceiling for answers.

Glancing at Mia, I saw that she was losing interest in nursing, which wasn't unusual, teething or not. She had less stamina on the second side, always. "Want me to take her?"

"Hmm?" Grace looked at me, then Mia. "Oh yeah, looks like she's topped off for now." She passed her over as she adjusted her top. "Thanks for talking to me about this."

"Does it help?" I slid off the bed with Mia in my arms as she cooed, then did a lap, rubbing her back. She let out a good one and tucked her little head into my neck as I kept walking around the room.

"Yeah, I think so." Grace pulled her legs up, wrapping her arms around her shins as she watched me. "It makes me feel less alone in this."

I stopped, swaying side to side while I patted Mia's bottom, which usually knocked her out. "Is there any reason you didn't tell me how you were feeling before?"

"Honestly?" Grace rested her chin on a knee. "I felt like

I should know how to be a mom instinctively. I guess it surprised me that not everything with parenting came naturally. I did love her immediately, which I know for some women—especially when dealing with postpartum—isn't always true. And part of me felt like I should just appreciate our healthy baby and deal with everything."

Damn, there's a lot of pressure on women. Men too, but this was another level. "I'm sorry you were going through this on your own."

"Thanks, but I should have said something. That's on me."

I turned my back to Grace. "Is she out?"

"She is."

I looked back over my shoulder. "We didn't give her any meds. Want me to wake her?"

Grace shook her head. "Nah. Maybe she doesn't need it. We can if she's struggling tonight."

I noted the confidence she had now with her decisions. Maybe she wasn't where she wanted to be, but she was getting there day by day. "Mom said she's on duty tonight. I'll go put Mia in the crib and let Mom know Tylenol is an option if she gets fussy again."

"Sounds good. I'll wait up for you." Grace gave me a look that was shy and filled with a longing that I was familiar with at the same time.

My body heated at that comment, but I worked to play it cool because I wanted Grace to take the lead, which meant not putting any pressure or expectations on her. Instead, my tongue skimmed my lip as I looked her way and whispered, "I'd like that" before hustling to Mia's room and praying for a smooth transfer with her staying zonked out. Surely that wouldn't be too much to ask for.

Chapter 9

Candlelight Confessions

***G**race*
I turned off the overhead lights in our bedroom while I debated candles, table lamps, or complete darkness. Did I leave my current playlist on or go for silence? Would Aidan consider Jason Isbell and the 400 Unit good music for our first time reconnecting? Were we having sex? Was this all too much? Not enough?

Good Lord, it had been ages since we'd had sex, but I wasn't a virgin here, though you wouldn't know that from the way my heart was racing.

This was insanity. *Calm all the way down, Grace.* Small steps. I had this. I did.

Let's see… I like candles. I lit the one on my side table and decided to turn off the table lamps. Low lighting seemed to be the way to go here. The light from the flames flickered on the ceiling, and the cinnamon-spiced-vanilla scent gave me a sense of calm. I was fine. This was fine.

I mean, a large part of me wanted to grab my phone and text Maggie. Was the first time after having a baby painful?

I'd had a C-section, so not quite the same there, though that recovery had been anything but pain free.

Good Lord, thinking of my recovery reminded me of the time at the hospital when Aidan had accidentally said something that made me laugh and I thought I might pass out from the sharp pain that had ripped through my abdominals. A small pillow had become my best friend, putting pressure on my belly anytime I moved, laughed on accident, et cetera.

But now my doctor had cleared me for intercourse *whenever I felt ready*. And I did, kind of, but part of me also felt like I'd never be ready.

What if I leaked?

What if I didn't get aroused?

What if my body turned Aidan off?

What if I couldn't orgasm?

I stood, paralyzed by indecision, next to my side table. Should I put on lingerie? Did any of it even fit anymore? Was this even what Aidan wanted tonight? What if he was tired and just wanted his mom to watch the baby so we could rest? Had I read him wrong?

Before I could continue my spiral, the door opened and Aidan slid in, locking it behind him before turning to face me. And there I was, still as a statue, stuck standing by our bed.

"Grace?" His face was creased with worry as he crossed quickly to my side. "What is it?" He pulled me against him, and I relaxed into his embrace. Surely he could feel my heart thumping through my thin tank, but the softness of his flannel and his familiar scent gave me comfort.

"I'm afraid." It took all that I had in me to whisper those words and not break eye contact, but it was worth it because

Aidan's face softened as he leaned forward and pressed a kiss to my forehead.

"It seems tonight is the night for talks—lots of them." He stepped over to our bed, pulling back the flannel duvet decked out in candy canes that I hadn't been able to resist buying. It made our bedroom look like Christmas—the duvet, the red flannel checked bedding, red berries in a white vase, and a green wreath above our bed.

My parents hadn't been big decorators for holidays. Still weren't. They said they had too much to do with semester finals at the university. Which I always knew came first. And honestly, for most holidays I was fine with no decor, except Christmas. Before Mia, I'd been a little over the top. Now, well, let's just say that if I didn't rein it in, we'd need a storage shed soon.

It helped focusing on my holiday decor and not the man I loved stripping down to his black boxer briefs and sliding into our bed. Damn. He was gorgeous. That tan skin taut over his abdominals made my core feel electrified. Why was I freaking out again?

Aidan lay down and pulled me into bed, then braced himself on an elbow as he scanned my face. What he was looking for, I wasn't sure. I was still in my pajama pants and tank, but I could feel the heat of his body seeping through the fabric. He looked at me with endless patience, which I knew to be true. Part of me thought we should just jump into some foreplay and see how it went—maybe that would be easier. The damn man wanted to talk—more—and I felt vulnerable and exposed already.

He pressed another kiss to my temple, which made me melt. "So... Afraid, huh? Let's talk about that."

I rolled to my back with a huff. Staring at the ceiling was easier. "Where do you want to start?"

"How about the beginning." He lay down, shoulder to shoulder with me, on his back. That helped somehow, not looking at him for this conversation.

"Um, well see, we haven't had sex for four months." Yep, if I'd had on my Apple watch, I would for sure have gotten a high-heart-rate notification.

"You don't say." His voice was filled with amusement. It would have stressed me out more if he hadn't snaked his pinky finger over to hook into mine. Somehow that little touch gave me confidence. "Babe, lay it on me. I'm well aware of our timeline. What are you worried about?"

I took a deep breath, then let it all out, one fear after another, rolling through them until my chest was heaving and silence filled the room. Well, along with Isbell singing "Cover Me Up" about his wife in the song that always made me cry. I guess all relationships had highs and lows.

"That it?" Aidan asked, squeezing my pinky.

"Is that it? Isn't that a lot?" My breath still wasn't even.

He rolled, letting go of my hand to hook a leg over my lower body and pull me to him. "Let's hit those concerns—all valid babe—one at a time. One, if this hurts, we stop and figure it out. Two, if you leak, you leak."

I winced.

"Gracie, I'm not grossed out or anything. If it makes you feel better, you can leave on your tank or I can grab a towel, but sex is messy. And I've read about sex after kids and sex while nursing. I'm betting you'll get aroused, but I'm not some delusional hero in one of your romance books. I'm well aware that aroused doesn't always mean wet and wet doesn't always mean aroused, so we can use lube."

I felt the flush from my belly to my chest to my cheeks. "*Aidan,*" I whispered, meeting his gaze.

"Just saying, Gracie, we have options. Lube's great.

Moving on. I'm pretty sure I can get you to orgasm, but if I can't, you've got toys and I know how to use them. Or if having that as a goal is too much, we can just have fun, and if we orgasm, cool; if not, we spent time together."

My heart rate was approaching normal levels. I mean, in my chest, but the pulse in my core was beating out its own rhythm and speaking up to say it was on board with some activity tonight.

"As for not being attracted to you in this body of yours that has had some changes. No. Fucking. Way."

I turned to watch the dancing flame, breaking contact with his heated look. The flickering candle made it hard to see his eyes fully, but I knew they were locked on me, and looking straight on was just too difficult.

I found my voice even if it wavered. "I'm just saying my belly isn't the same. And my boobs are big and sometimes wet. And the stretch marks won't ever be going away..."

Aidan rolled over me, pinning me under him. "Grace Vivian Kane Russo—"

"I didn't keep my maiden name."

"Don't care. You need all the names right now." He brushed my hair back from my eyes, pressed a kiss to my lips, and then leaned down to whisper into my ear like he wanted the message to sink in deep. "Woman, you are gorgeous." His warm breath against my ear and neck gave me goose bumps. "You were before you had Mia, you are now, you will be if and when we have more children. I am attracted to *you*"—he pressed an open-mouthed kiss to my neck—"the you that you are inside. The stuff on the outside is just decoration. I love the you who sings like a fool in the kitchen, dancing with Baxter."

I choked out a laugh even though tears were welling up and I was powerless to stop them.

Aidan was not deterred. "I'm crazy about the woman who is fanatical about finding more money to help run the programs at the library. The person you are when you're fired up about topics you're passionate about brings me to my knees."

"Fuck the patriarchy," I whispered.

"Bring on the matriarchy," he whispered back.

"I love your loyalty, your passion, your kindness. Watching you with Mia makes me know with complete certainty that she's the luckiest girl in the world to be raised by you. And whether you are the size and shape you were, are, or whatever you become, seeing you in a wrap dress with boots will never fail to make me hard."

Tears were free-falling down my face. "I love you so much." My throat felt raw, but so did my soul.

Aidan pulled up to look at me, balancing on his elbows so that his thumbs could wipe away my tears. "Back at you, babe. I love you more than you will ever imagine."

I attempted a bit of deflection. This was getting heavy. "So do you want to heat up these sheets with me?" I asked with a small smile.

He sat looking at my face for a few beats of my heart where I couldn't read his expression, but the vibe he gave was that he saw my change of topic and was deciding if he should call me on it.

He leaned down and pressed a soft kiss to my mouth. Just as I parted my lips to deepen the kiss, he pulled back. "I absolutely want that if, and only if, that is truly what you want. Did we hit all your concerns? Is there anything else you want to talk about, or do you have another topic change in you tonight?"

I shook my head, meeting his grin. In this position, I felt surrounded by Aidan. And in actuality I was. But it was more than that. It was like he'd cushioned all of me. I didn't know how to explain it except to say I felt safe, the most at ease I'd been since before we conceived Mia. Like it was the two of us again and we were here for each other. Why had I allowed that distance to get between us? We were better together. I remembered his words earlier when we were taking the family picture.

"Aidan Edward Russo"—I pecked his lips—"I'm wrapped up in you too, or in us. And while I'm not where I want to be confidence wise, I'm ready to work on getting there. So yes, I want to burn up these sheets while we keep noise to a minimum, not only because I want to keep Mia asleep as long as possible but also because I have to face your mother tomorrow."

"You're in?"

I gave him a scalding look. "More like I'd like you to be in... me."

He burst out laughing, letting his head drop to my shoulder as his weight settled on me. "Jesus, that was bad, Gracie."

"But truthful, Russo." I gave a playful slap to his butt. "Let's get this party started."

Chapter 10

Hair Trigger

A*idan*

Candlelight danced over Grace's tearstained cheeks. I didn't love seeing her cry, but there was a lightness to her that I hadn't seen since prepregnancy. Heck, since before we started trying to get pregnant, when we'd thought everything would just happen the first time with no worries. How naive we'd been.

"So, Ms. Russo, this is a go?" I leaned down to press a kiss to the crook of her neck. She'd loved that before, and I was assuming it hadn't changed.

She immediately tilted her head to give me more access as murmurs of pleasure fell from her mouth. Hmm, I'd say we were on the right track. But...

"Words, Gracie."

"Get going, Russo. I already said yes."

Sassy Grace was back. I liked it. That was a good sign.

I pulled back, rolled to the side of the bed, and stood up. Grace gave me a noise of protest, which only made my cock get more interested in the night's schedule. Part of me was kicking myself. Why hadn't we just made out over the past four months? Sex didn't have to always be the finish line, and that might have helped us connect when that distance had crept in. Hindsight and all.

She propped herself up on her elbows, looking at me standing to her side. "Where do you think you're going?"

"Need to grab some stuff and need you to shed those pajamas. The tank is optional, as we discussed."

I headed into our en suite, steps from the bed, grabbed what I needed, and kept talking to her. "I'm glad to do it for you or"—I made it back to the bed, noting her pants kicked to the floor—"you can take care of it."

"Done." She smirked. "What did you need to get?"

I held up the lube and a hand towel. Even in the low light from the flame, I saw her cheeks get rosy again. "Gracie, we talked about this. Whatever you need, I'm here for it. I just want you to be comfortable."

I tossed the two items on the mattress to her side, climbing back next to her because I couldn't take one more moment that she wasn't in my arms. Damn, I wanted her to know how attracted to her I was. I couldn't care less if she leaked or if we needed to find ways to make sex comfortable. She was nothing but arousing to me, and I had a feeling we just needed to go ahead with this and her confidence would follow as she saw that I was anything but turned off by her. Maybe I just needed to make her laugh.

"Didn't you tell me one of the romances you read for book club had an adult breastfeeding scene? Want to do a little role playing?" I grinned, pressing kisses to her neck as I worked to fight back my laughter, knowing what her reaction would be.

I wasn't disappointed.

"Aidan." She squirmed under me. "No, I mean, just no. Lisa Kleypas's books are amazing, but a big hell no."

"No kink shaming here, babe. Promise." I was rewarded with her muffled laughter as she pressed her face into my chest, trying to keep from being too loud.

After a beat, she relaxed in my arms and tipped her head back to meet my eyes. "Thanks."

I brushed her hair back. "For what?"

"Trying to help me relax."

"Did it work?" She was so damn beautiful, her gaze soft as she looked at me with want, which I was there for.

"Think so," she whispered as she brought her hands up to pull my head to hers. Our mouths meeting, the kiss deepened faster than I could've imagined as a hunger for my wife overwhelmed me. She nipped at my lower lip, tugging it into her mouth and sucking at it before she moved along my jaw to bite the lobe of my ear.

I worked to stay in the moment, ignoring my body's desire to hurry. No, that would not do. Nothing wrong with fast sex sometimes as long as Grace came first, but not today, not this time.

I paid attention to her body, and Grace was everywhere. Her hands slid from my hair, to my back, to inside my boxer briefs. One of her legs was wrapped around mine, pulling me to her core as she ground against my cock. Yeah, getting aroused wasn't going to be an issue she was dealing with today.

As my mouth moved down her neck to the top of her boobs, I paused. "Do you want me to skip your breasts completely?" I knew being blunt might cause her to get embarrassed again, but better to ask than fuck this up.

She paused, one hand on my ass. "Um, how about avoiding the nipples?"

I loved how she phrased it like a question, as if she wasn't sure. I didn't give a fuck if milk was all over us. I mean, she was a superhero, first carrying our baby and keeping her healthy, now nourishing her with milk she produced. I thought it was amazing.

But moving on. I'd avoid her nipples for now even though they were hard under the cotton, begging for attention. I figured I'd just leave the tank as is and kiss the rest of her breasts through it. Maybe that would be the most comfortable for Grace for the first time. I knew she'd mentioned that her boobs were more sensitive than usual, so I moved gently, tracing with my tongue across her cleavage, then around the side with open-mouthed kisses, continuing down to her belly.

"Aidan," she moaned, making my body alight with desire. Damn, I hadn't wanted to pressure her, but God, I'd missed her. It wasn't sex—though that was great—it was the connection to the woman I loved more than anything. It was the closeness I felt when we were together.

"Yeah, babe?" I nosed her tank up a little, placing kisses, nips, and more across her belly, working to keep her feeling good.

"I haven't even gotten my hands on you," she whispered, her legs pushing in on either side of me, a good sign I was on the right path.

"Beg to differ, Gracie—your hands have been all over me." I sucked on a patch of her belly near her C-section scar. God, I didn't want to think about that right now. I'd freaked way the fuck out when she had to go in for that surgery but had tried to remain outwardly calm. Thank God I was allowed to go with her. I would have melted down otherwise, but talk about powerless. I was grateful for this reminder in the form of a dark line across her pubic bone that my wife was a badass and deserved an orgasm, if possible, right now.

"I mean, you know..."

I bit back a snort. "I'm sorry, Grace, did you become bashful? Are you referring to my dick?"

"I mean, yeah?" She was breathless, so I was done with this conversation. The woman was trying to be unselfish when I wanted this to be all about her.

I fought for patience. "Grace, if you touch me, it's going to be all over. Four months, remember—I'm on a hair trigger over here. Let me make this good for you for a while, and then we can have the fastest sex in history because I'm so aroused by you I will not last long. Cool?"

She giggled, which was a sound I'd missed. Glad she was good with me laying it out there. "Go ahead."

I continued down, tugging her underwear off and tossing them somewhere behind me. It didn't matter where. Mine were staying on to give me the smallest bit of control over myself until I got her there.

I'd told her we didn't have to make orgasms the goal for the night, and we didn't. But my logic here was that she was worried about arousal, and I'd read about how hormones fucked with lubrication. I figured if I could get her there with my mouth, maybe that wouldn't stress her out as much as manual stimulation. Lube was fine, but we were starting here, and then who knew where we'd end up. It was zero hardship to find out, that was for damn sure.

Once I settled between her legs, she tossed her legs over my shoulders. I sucked at the sensitive skin of her inner thighs, rubbing the stubble on my face over her legs as I looked up in the flickering light at this woman I loved. The thought that came to me over and over was how damn lucky I was that she was mine and I was hers. Her gaze on me said she was here for this.

"Still good?"

"So good." She panted. "Don't stop."

"Never," I promised.

I lowered my mouth and placed a kiss to her core, which had the immediate effect of making her hips lift as she moaned, pleasure rolling through her body. I debated telling her to keep it down—I knew she didn't want Mia and my mom to hear anything—but fuck it. I didn't want her trying to limit herself. Mia would survive—Mom would grab her if she woke. And my mom was ridiculously sex positive, and I couldn't imagine she'd say anything to Grace. Me, on the other hand, I was sure she'd make some crack.

Moving on.

I stroked my tongue up from her opening to her clit, twirling my tongue around it and pressing light sucks to that little button of nerves. Grace couldn't hold back, her hips moving mindlessly as her breath came in short gasps and she moaned. I lost time in her, continuing the pressure on her core as I eventually slid in a finger, then two, paying close attention to how she reacted. She was close. I could feel the small flutters of her walls.

Focusing on her clit, I kept the pattern consistent as I watched her writhe with desire above me, need flooding my body as I held off my own orgasm, waiting for her to tip over that edge. With a few more strokes of my tongue and one with a finger, she finally came and her legs clenched around my shoulders as she cried out with a beautiful moan. I slowed down the pressure on her core as I held my tongue against her clit until her body became boneless with a sigh worthy of the weeks and months we'd lost. I followed her body back up, kissing my love into every spot I could find before I moved to capture her mouth in a hard kiss.

We kissed and kissed and kissed until I pulled back to

check in and looked at her in awe. "You are so damn beautiful."

"Remember that I told you to get in me, Russo." She wagged her eyebrows at me.

I shook my head, laughter in my voice. "I aim to please, ma'am."

"Then let's get pleasing some more."

Sliding off her, I got out of the bed to kick off my underwear and grab a vibrator from the bedside table where I knew she stored it and prayed to all that was holy that it was charged.

She gave me a skeptical look. "Um, not sure if you were paying attention, but I just orgasmed. I don't have to during sex—you know that."

"I don't give a fuck; we might just have fun with it." I slid back into the bed next to her. "And for this first time, I'm voting we go the slippery route."

I poured some lube onto my fingers, knowing she'd been concerned about pain the first time, and I wanted zero chance of that. I slid some gently into her and also coated my cock with it. Bottle to the table, thankful for the hand towel, we were ready to go.

"Position preference, sexy?" I said as I placed another kiss to her neck. She didn't say anything, so I pulled back to see her face. She was watching me, a look of wonder visible.

"Babe?"

I could tell her eyes were a bit watery, which hadn't been the case a moment ago, and that made me worry. "Are you okay? We can stop if that's all you want to do tonight. Whatever—"

Grace pushed a finger against my mouth. "No. You are just showing me once again tonight that you were made for me."

She pushed my shoulder, and I let her lead as she rolled me to my back and then swung a leg over my hips and grabbed my cock to hold in position as she slowly slid down.

As she did, she looked down at me. "Thanks for being amazing about this."

I placed my hands on her hips and watched as she tentatively rose and then lowered above me, letting her set the pace and depth.

"Gracie?"

"Hmm?"

"You're hot as fuck." I squeezed her hip in my hand. "And I'm all in for cowgirl position. Anytime, any day."

She tossed her head back as she laughed, still rolling her hips as her thighs squeezed my body. Damn, she was a goddess.

"Aidan," she said, speeding up a bit.

"Um-hmm," I said, watching her go.

"Love you," she whispered as she began to chase her own pleasure, bringing me right along with her as she cried out again and let go.

Chapter 11

Santa Comes Down the Chimney

Grace

As we walked up the sidewalk to Logan and Allyson's beautiful home, I was distracted by the fit of Aidan's jeans. Last night had been wonderful. I'd felt cherished, listened to. I hadn't realized how much our lack of sex life in the past few months could be contributed to the amount of fear and anxiety I was carrying around about it. By sharing that with Aidan, I felt like it wasn't only my "issue" anymore but one we were working on together. Who knew communication could do so much? Um, I'm pretty sure everyone, that's who.

One thing I was struggling with now was trying to think back to when just telling Aidan how I was feeling hadn't become second nature. Was it when we got pregnant? Was it before? Had we gotten so used to being together over the years that we stopped working on making sure were actually *there* for each other?

Whenever it was, last night had been amazing. As had the middle of the night. And this morning. And the shower before we came here. We hadn't had sex every time—we'd just been wrapped up in each other. Kisses, caresses, mutual orgasms, the more we touched, the more I wanted to. And now I was back to noticing my man's ass. It was pretty nice. Heck, when he'd come out of our closet in his fitted forest-green Henley, jeans, and boots, I'd wanted to suggest skipping this gathering altogether, but it was Logan and Allyson's first holiday party. I knew it was a big deal to the two of them. When Sophia had heard about the party and how we were looking for a babysitter, she decided to stay for another night even though we'd been told we could take Mia.

When Logan moved to Highland Falls years ago, he'd been so grief-stricken over the loss of his first wife that he'd sort of closed himself off from the world. His friendship with Allyson had blossomed over the past year to something more. Now they were married with a baby on the way.

Their house was outside town, near Highland Woods, where Logan was the park director. The cabin was lit up with large windows open to the road, and I could see our friends gathering inside. Luckily the winter temperatures had the ground frozen because there was a creek bed you had to drive over when coming up the lane. That bed was dry though and super shallow when it wasn't.

At the door we headed right on in, knowing that none of our friends stood on formality—you knocked once as you were walking in and shouted hello. Conversations filled the air, as did a low level of music that was, if I wasn't mistaken, the Avett Brothers. I deposited my coat on one of the wall hooks near the door before Aidan and I headed to the kitchen to add our cooler bag to the lineup of the others from the guests already here. Levi was standing at the island, looking from the coolers already in the kitchen to ours.

"Is this a small-town thing?" he said to Aidan, pointing to the collection.

"Hmm?" Aidan asked, not following.

Levi nodded to the plethora of coolers. "You all don't trust the host to have something to drink so you bring your own?"

"Not sure if that's a small-town thing, a Midwest thing, or just a common-sense one. I feel like it started with our friends in college, though that was often a case of cheap beer back then. No one ever had a ton of cash, so we'd bring whatever we wanted to drink. Now we just bring what we know we like but are happy to share with others if they need something." Aidan shrugged, looking at me as if to confirm his thoughts.

I nodded my agreement.

Sully leaned over across the island. "Yeah, Jake and I brought growlers from the brewery." He pointed to a setup by the fridge.

Glancing at the island, I noticed the platters of food. I'd brought the bacon-bites appetizer that Max always devoured, but I saw charcuterie boards, dips, some veggie trays, and enough desserts that we would all be in a sugar coma if we ate everything. The scent from the oven told me Allyson was making her pizza dip, which made my mouth water.

I looked over the food to Levi, thinking about his comment. "I think it's kind of like this food." I gestured at my appetizer. "When you host this crew, you're opening your home to a large group. The host always has food and drinks, but we all also bring stuff to make it a little easier for them."

Max walked by, gave me a fist bump, and grabbed two pinwheels of the cream-cheese-bacon-crescent-roll goodness. His mumbled thanks around the mouthful of food made me laugh as he headed back to talk to Drew Spencer by the fireplace.

"So what you're telling me is that I can grab a beer from any of those?" Levi gestured with a thumb over his shoulder to the bags against the wall.

"Or the growler, or the drinks in the fridge, or pour a glass of wine—"

"—Or Irish whiskey, or bring your own beverages, you freeloader you." Logan came up beside his twin with a smirk. "Highland Falls social etiquette stumping you?"

"Doesn't take much to stump the lesser twin." Maeve, Allyson's sister, joined our group.

Aidan leaned over, his mouth brushing my ear as he whispered, "This is about to get good."

I nodded, trying to keep my smile to myself as a shiver went down my back at the contact. Aidan and I had been placing bets on what was going on between those two. Levi moved to Highland Falls from the suburbs this past April. Logan had been a resident for at least three years, so I'm not sure what made Levi decide now was the time to move down to join his brother, but his move caused a chain reaction and the Traub parents had recently moved down too.

Maeve, Allyson's sister, wasn't a resident yet, and I couldn't imagine her becoming one. She'd visited for the first time this spring and bounced in and out of town since then. Allyson said she never settled in one place for long. Neither one of the Murphy sisters were close to their parents, who lived on the East Coast, but the two of them were determined to see each other more now. And whenever Maeve came to town, she and Levi clashed like oil and water. Or so it seemed. In Levi's case, I felt like it was one of those *protests too much* situations. Time would tell, but I strongly believed there was some attraction simmering just below the surface.

Maeve was corralled by Allyson though, so no fireworks show for us.

Levi joined Aidan and me with his own drink and snagged a bacon bite. He moaned around a mouthful. "Damn, this is good."

"And ridiculously easy to make," I pointed out. "If you want the recipe, let me know."

"Maybe I just need to follow you around to parties," he said with a smirk.

"That's what I do," Max called over.

"Thanks, guys," I leaned over and pressed a kiss to Aidan's cheek. "I'm going to go talk to some of the girls."

He squeezed my waist as I moved past him and off to join Maggie and Emma.

As I headed in their direction, I glanced around the large cabin, stopping to talk to a few small groups as I moved through the room. Logan and Allyson's great room was gorgeous with a living room and kitchen running the back of the cabin and a wall of windows facing the woods. The deck off the back had chairs that faced the woods and white lights lit up the winter night, showing off the snow coating the branches of the trees and giving some ambience to the firepit and Adirondacks in the yard. Aidan and Levi caught my eye as they headed through the french doors to join Sully by the fire just off the porch.

Bringing my focus back into the house, I reached the large media lounger Maggie and Emma were reclining on in the corner of the living room. The two of them had their heads together as Emma sipped on some LaCroix and Maggie held a mug in her hand. They had a perfect location to see what was going on outside by the firepit and inside in the great room, which was not surprising considering Maggie's desire to be in the know with all that was happening.

"Saved you a spot, Grace," Maggie said, patting the seat as I slid onto the lounger with them.

I gave a brief moment of gratitude to my change of dress for the night. I'd almost worn another wrap dress since Aidan had mentioned how much he enjoyed them last night, but then in our group text thread, Allyson said they were planning on using the firepit for those who wanted to head outside, so I'd chosen dark skinny jeans tucked into tall boots, a white fitted sweater, and a red plaid scarf. I felt like it was festive without being over the top. Maggie and Emma had clearly gotten the message too as they were both in leggings and longer sweaters.

"Thanks for the spot," I said, kicking back and relaxing into the down cushions.

"Do you need a drink?" Emma looked from me to search for Max, I'm sure to tell him to go get me what I needed.

I placed a hand on her arm. "No, nothing needed yet. I haven't decided if I'm having a drink and doing a whole 'pump and dump' situation tonight or sticking to water."

"The things you never knew you'd need to consider, am I right?" Maggie said, raising her glass. "I'm grateful I have some time before I need to think about that again because this warm cider and salted-caramel whisky is delicious."

Damn, that did sound good.

Maggie waved her beverage in a circle toward my face. "Are we addressing the clear aura you have going on that says your sex drought is over, or are we ignoring that tonight?"

"Jeez, Mags." Emma shook her head.

"I'm just saying I'm glad to see it."

I didn't need a mirror to know my cheeks were now red, but I simply looked at Emma and Maggie and gave a slow nod.

Maggie motioned her hand in a tell-me-more gesture.

"She does not need to elaborate, Mags. Especially in the middle of this party."

"Note, we are not in the middle but tucked over to the side, out of hearing range of everyone but ourselves," Maggie said to Emma, then looked my way. "I mean, don't share if you don't want to, but last time we talked, this was long overdue. Feeling okay about everything?"

I glanced around, ensuring that Maggie was right and there was no one nearby. "Yeah, I'm feeling great."

"What made the difference?"

"We finally talked, and Aidan reassured me about a lot of fears that I hadn't even realized I was feeling."

Maggie nodded sagely. "Communication—it is, sadly, all that it's cracked up to be."

"Yeah, I should have had the conversation so long ago." I rubbed my hands on my jeans, filled with a bit of nervous energy. "I have no idea why I stopped confiding in him."

"Because shit gets real when a baby comes into your home." Maggie hopped up and started walking around the lounger, her hands moving as she spoke.

Emma leaned over. "Prepare yourself—this is one of her soapbox issues."

Oh boy.

Maggie ignored both of us and gathered steam as she spoke. "I mean, we have these baby showers. People want to guess the candy bar in a diaper which, I mean, eww." Her face was priceless with her nose wrinkled in disgust. "They give these parenting books out that talk about sleep training and attachment parenting versus other types of parenting. People talk about formula feeding, breastfeeding, cloth diapers, disposables. Food introduction is gone over in detail, as is childproofing your house. But riddle me this— why doesn't anyone talk about the emotional roller coaster you go on as a mom after having a baby? Why aren't there articles written on how your entire pelvic region is rearranged? Why doesn't anyone talk about sex after pregnancy or how your vision of yourself changes, or how hard it is to just take a moment to breathe? Or possibly the benefits of seeing a pelvic floor therapist after baby? Hmm?" She stopped trying to wear a hole in the floor and turned to face us with her hands on her hips as she waited for our response.

Emma and I muttered in unison, "Patriarchy."

Maggie threw up her hands. "Exactly." With that, she plopped down beside us. "I'm sorry, Grace. I feel like I wasn't up front with you about the journey into motherhood. I failed as a friend."

"Add me to that list."

I looked up to see Ivy moving to join us, a glass of ice water in her hand. Our bookstore-owning friend had a fashion style more out of the days of Woodstock than the current time period and was clearly ignoring any idea of standing outside that night. Her blond hair was down and loose with curls cascading over her shoulder to the red dress she wore. I loved it even if I didn't think I could pull it off. I was a fan of the wrap dress because of the simplicity. Hers was a sheer dress with a plunging neckline that my current cup size would overwhelm. There was dark red embroidery in key locations all over, and judging by the look on Jake's face as she slid next to me on the lounger, I'd say he was a fan.

I bumped her shoulder with my own. "Hey, lady, I haven't seen you since your new babe arrived. How are you doing?" I worked closely with Ivy when we wanted to do author visits in town and the library and bookstore joined forces to foot the bill.

"We're good, thanks. And thanks for sending dinner home last week with Jake."

"I wish I could take credit for that, but Aidan made the chicken pasta for you all. I just made the brownies."

"Grateful either way. But"—she looked at Mags and Emma, then back to me—"I couldn't help but overhear Mags, which isn't hard when she's on a roll. I should have said something to you too, but it's almost like you forget how hard it is the further away you get from it. I will say from zero kids to one was far harder than one to two if that helps any."

"Really?" I gave Ivy an assessing glance. That seemed hard to believe. Then again, when she had Addie, she'd been a single mom. That alone made me feel incapable. Like, think how many single moms there were out there, killing it, and I'd spiraled when I had a husband to help.

"I see you," she said, leaning back on an elbow on the mountain of pillows. "You're judging yourself."

"Again." Maggie wagged an eyebrow at me.

I looked to Emma, waiting for her to gang up on me too.

She raised her hands in protest. "I'm not saying anything. I'm not even in this mothering club yet; I'm just soaking in all the wisdom before it's my turn."

"I don't know." I sighed, turning to watch Aidan out the window and wishing, at least part of me, that we were home. "I guess I look at single moms like you were, Ivy, and wonder why I couldn't hack it as easily."

"It wasn't easy for me either," she says. "For sure, one

reason it's easier this time around is the fact that Jake is with me. But don't compare your inner struggles with what you see from others' outward appearance. It's enough to acknowledge that it's hard for us all."

"You're right," I mumbled.

"Okay, now that we have that discussion over with, what is the status of daycare for Miss Mia," Ivy asked. "I did reach out to Teri, our daycare provider, but she doesn't have any openings until a year from now for an infant."

"I asked Anna," Maggie said.

"What?" I glanced from Maggie to Emma. "I don't want your mom thinking I'm pressuring her to start running a daycare."

Emma laughed. "You should know by now that my mom can't be pressured into much."

True. I'd gotten to know Anna at the library. She'd joined many of our book clubs over the years, and the woman knew her own mind. Still, I felt a twinge of embarrassment like I was somehow at fault for not having daycare figured out for my baby.

Maggie nodded to Emma before looking back at me. "At any rate, Anna said that wasn't something she could handle right now but recommended I call Kris at our daycare because Anna heard through the Lou Williams' grapevine that the Harper family was moving to Tennessee to be closer to their family."

My heart skipped a beat. There was only one Harper family I knew of in town. They came into the library for story time on Saturdays, and they had one of the infant slots at the preschool/ daycare on the farm where Maggie's daughter El went.

I turned big eyes to Mags. "You didn't hear it on your own?"

"Kris hasn't said anything, so I'm checking into it. Anna just said something when we dropped El off to come here."

It felt too dangerous to hope, but Lou was plugged into all the gossip in town, so that was promising. Was there a way to find daycare in town without having to give up my career or drive an hour a day to a bigger city or some other plan that we hadn't thought of yet? I guess I'd have to wait a little longer to find out.

"So..." Ivy scanned me from head to toe with a positively wicked grin. "Looks like you finally had Santa come down your chimney, Grace. Or maybe more accurately, come up it?"

We all paused as we processed Ivy's comment and then promptly burst into a fit of laughter.

Emma shook her head. "Maggie has been such a bad influence on you, Ivy." To which Ivy and Maggie high-fived across me.

As much as a quiet night home with my family sounded appealing, some time with these girls was just what I needed. I felt more like *me* than I had in some time.

Chapter 12

Flying Free

A *idan*

The cold temps had given the air a crisp feeling that I associated with winter in Illinois. I mean, I had grown up only a few hours away. To be fair, maybe this wasn't unique to Illinois or even the Midwest, but in my mind, this was how a December night should be.

The flame from the fire was throwing off heat as it devoured the logs in the Solo Stove. While the air was chilly, with my flannel over my Henley, I wasn't too cold but exactly right. The fire danced and I stared, lost in thought.

"You good, man?" Levi came up to me, passing over a beer.

As I took it, I gave the label a second glance. It wasn't one of the ones we'd brought but a West Coast IPA from the Homestead called Fire & Rain that they often brewed around the holidays. Worked for me.

I looked back to the fire, wondering where to start. "I'm good. Just wrapping my brain around a few things."

Max's voice brought me back to the yard. "How can we help?"

A look up told me the male contingent of this party was joining us at the firepit. Max, Jake, Drew, and Logan came to stand next to Levi, Sully, and me.

"You all get kicked out?" I asked with a glance back to the house. A second look showed someone dancing. Looking closer, it was Maggie—no shock there—and possibly Ivy?

"Maggie was taking over the music situation," Logan said.

"Great," Sully said. "The woman hasn't had more than a drink for over a year."

"She's had at least two of those apple ciders," Jake said.

"Three," Max replied.

"Shit," Sully said.

Noting his grin, I knew he wasn't actually upset.

"So, young padawan, how can we be of service?" Drew stood tall, attempting to project an air of superiority, which was squashed when Jake immediately knocked his brother upside the head.

That was pretty much par for the course with these two. Heck, Logan and Levi weren't much better. And Max and Sully might as well be siblings. It all made me miss Declan more than I could say.

Jake stepped closer to me. "Let's see, last time we talked, you were having a severe lack of 'spicy times' at your house and were worried you might hurt Grace, right?"

"I thought the *spicy* code word was just because the kids were with us," Logan said.

"I like it." Levi gave me a wink.

"Bet you do," Logan said.

"Jesus." I rubbed a hand over my face. "Okay, let's get this out before anyone else joins us. I was worried, but we did talk about it and that helped."

"And things"—Jake cleared his throat—"have improved?"

I let out a little laugh and shook my head. "Spice levels have risen, yes."

"But…," Max prodded.

"But I've got a lot on my mind. My mom pointed out some stuff I hadn't noticed. And then the daycare we'd planned on using fell through, and we're scrambling to figure out what we're doing come January."

"Shit," Logan murmured.

"Damn, man, I'm sorry." Levi looked at me from across the fire.

"Any leads?" Jake asked.

"Nope. But we'll figured this out," I said.

Levi held his can up and I knocked mine against it.

The door to the back porch opened, and Maggie stuck her head out. "Boys, why are you all standing around a firepit when you could be dancing?"

"She's all yours, man," Max said to Sully with a wide smile visible even in that beard of his.

Sully shot a finger his way as he headed to the house, calling to Maggie, "Babe, are you done with the whiskey?"

Maggie immediately stepped out onto the porch with her hands on her hips.

"Uh-oh," Levi said next to me.

"Yep. That about sums up that situation," I said.

"Cole Sullivan, I'll have you know that I've had three drinks. Three!" She held up three fingers in his face as she looked up at him from her new vantage point on the porch, her voice easily carrying to us in the yard. Heck, if Logan had any neighbors, they'd hear this exchange too. "I'm tipsy but not drunk. And I don't appreciate your trying to rain on my parade here."

Sully let out a visible sigh as he stepped up to Maggie and, in my opinion, took his life in his hands as he pulled her to him. "Princess, I'm not trying to rain on anything. I just don't want you passed out tonight or hungover tomorrow when El is spending the night with my parents."

Maggie tilted her head as she considered his point. Then, with a tap to his chest, she said, "Good point. I'll have water until we leave, but for now, you all need to get your asses inside and we need to dance!" She grabbed Sully's hand and dragged him in behind her. The majority of the crew outside followed her in.

After a minute or so, Levi and I stood on our own. I was ready to go in, but something about his expression made me want to check in.

"You good, man?" I asked, repeating his question from earlier.

He looked up at me in surprise. "Yeah, why?"

"You looked stressed. Wanted to check."

He sighed, looking off into the woods. "Just a lot on my plate."

"Work?" I wasn't sure what else it could be.

"Yep. More work than hours in a day. Working for yourself is great until it isn't." He took another drink of his beer, then gestured to the house. "Want to head in?"

I agreed, turning to head up the steps, but paused when we hit the deck. "Sorry about the work, but let me know if I can help in any way. We could get out for a run tomorrow, or you can swing by for dinner one night next week if you just want to hang out, though you need to be cool with a baby."

"Man, that isn't a deterrent. And I haven't set eyes on Baxter the wonder pup lately."

"So both?" I asked as we stepped up to the door.

"Both. Run tomorrow around eleven?"

"You've got it." We bumped fists and walked inside.

My eyes immediately found Grace. She was standing with the girls and Tim, who had just come in with Eric. They were swaying with their arms around each other, belting out "Head Full of Doubt/ Road Full of Promise" from the Avett Brothers. Her smile was wide, her eyes shiny with what looked like a few tears. Even from here, I could tell that she was happy.

My heart was full. For the first time since Mia had been born, she looked like she was that bird and she was flying free.

Several hours later, we were bumping down the country road and headed back to town. The country roads were clear of snow, and the plowed snow-covered fields were white landscapes stretching out in every direction as far as the eye could see. The moon lit the night, and a freight train was slowly moving against the horizon several fields away.

"You have fun, babe?"

"So much." She was resting her head on the seat, her gaze on me.

"You need to pump as soon as we get home?" I asked, flipping on the blinker to head onto the main road into Highland. My mom should have Mia in bed, but if her gums were sore, they might be up. It wasn't too late, but it was past the little one's bedtime for sure.

She groaned, a hand to her breasts. "Yep, it just started to get bad. I only had one drink though, and it was several hours ago. If Mia's up, I can just feed her. Or I can store it up for later."

"You know it would have been okay if you wanted to drink more and dump the milk, right?" I asked, trying to gauge if this was a situation where she felt like she needed to set her desires aside again.

"I know. I really was fine not drinking." Her voice was quiet.

She turned away from me, so I squeezed her knee. "You good?"

Gracie kept her gaze trained out the window. "Yeah, I guess this is just one more thing we need to talk about that is about as 'unsexy as you can get.'"

What? I ran over her words in my brain before saying anything, hoping I didn't fuck any of this up. "Umm, what's unsexy?"

She dropped her head back on the headrest and looked to the ceiling of the truck. "Nursing? Pumping? Take your pick."

Another turn had us rolling down Main and pulling into our drive. I turned off the car and unbuckled, leaning over to do the same for Grace before placing a hand on her arm. "Gracie, look at me."

"I'd rather not."

"Gracie..."

"It's embarrassing, Aidan."

God, how had we stopped communicating for so many weeks? Months? I mean, I was glad we were now, but starting back up was tough. So many damn roadblocks.

"Didn't we go over this last night? There is nothing about you"—I squeezed her biceps—"*not a thing* that I find unsexy."

She refused to make eye contact. "Sure."

This woman. Stubborn didn't cover it, though I liked seeing her spunky side again. "Grace, like I said, no adult-lactation kink here, but I find you absolutely attractive when I see you nursing Mia. It's not like the nursing is sexy, but more that you, with your body, are making this baby of ours that you already grew *inside you* flourish on the outside. And again, you are doing that with *your body.* I mean, it's damn miraculous. I can't do that, don't you see?"

She was facing me now, tears streaming down her face as she listened.

"Women should rule the world because they created it and everyone in it. So yes, I find you sexy. Nursing, pumping, whatever. I am in awe of you, baby, and I wish like hell you could see it."

She leaned forward, pressing her lips to mine before sitting back in her seat. "Aidan Russo, I fucking love you."

My smile met hers. "That's awesome, Grace Russo, because I fucking love you too."

With that, we headed into the house where Mia was absolutely waiting up for us with some sore gums that would only be soothed by a little Tylenol and time with her mom.

As I closed up the house for the night, I heard Grace singing Miley Cyrus's "Used to be Young" and shook my head with a smile. She loved Miley and enjoyed expounding to anyone who would listen to her about how the media spun Miley's narrative to be a negative one. I poked my head in to tease her a bit but stopped when I saw the way she was looking at Mia as she serenaded her while Mia nursed. Mia's gaze was locked on Grace's, her hand on Grace's mouth. The love between the two of them was palpable and fucking beautiful.

My mom's words in mind, I silently slid my phone out of my back pocket and took a picture before backing out of the room. Many more to take to make up for the past few months, but I would do better for the two loves of my life. We had this.

Chapter 13

Holiday Glow

G*race*

I was wiped. The library had been a zoo. With two days until Christmas, parents had been in, stocking up on books for their little ones over the holidays. We had activity bags to go with different art projects for kids to do while at home with their families. Tim was a machine, handing out paper bags, reading to kids, and arguing with Aslan as she vocalized her displeasure for Tim daring to run out of treats for her. The nerve.

I kept busy finishing grants that had a deadline of year's end. With the bookstore and the school, we were working on a big grant that would run through the Library of Congress. It was a bit ambitious, but I thought we had a shot at it. We weren't as big as some of their award recipients in the past like First Book or Dolly's Imagination Library, but we were just as vital and in our rural area. Book access was an issue for some.

By the time I took a break after grant writing and filling in downstairs when Gabby had to leave, taking her opinionated feline with her, I realized it was the afternoon and my breakfast was a distant memory and lunch was past. I was just mentally taking an inventory on any food we had in the kitchen that wasn't loaded with sugar when the door opened and Allyson ducked inside.

"Hey, stranger," I called as she made her way to the circulation desk where I was standing with Tim.

Tim snorted at Allyson's T-shirt, which said I Run on Coffee and Christmas Cheer. "Nice shirt."

"Ditto," Allyson said, high-fiving Tim for his ugly Christmas sweatshirt that stated Don We Now Our Gay Apparel in rainbow colors.

"To what do we owe the pleasure of your presence?" I said, grateful for the lull so that I had a moment to visit with a friend before wrapping everything up for the day.

The library had limited hours for Christmas Eve. We were closed, of course, on Christmas. I was hoping to finish all I needed to do so that I could actually enjoy the next two days at home. Tim had volunteered to man the library tomorrow with Gabby, so I wouldn't be back in here until the twenty-sixth.

"A little birdy called the café and asked if we could do a delivery," Allyson said as she placed a bag on the counter.

Looking inside, I saw some of her wrap sandwiches, two side Caesars, and a variety of pastries and cookies.

"Score!" Tim said, pulling the buffet out on the desk.

I looked from the food to Allyson. "Aidan?"

"Got it in one," she said. "He called and said he knew you were swamped today and hadn't brought your lunch, but he was hung up in Champaign doing last-minute shopping with his mom before she headed back. I volunteered to bring some food by."

"You didn't have to do that," I said half-heartedly as I

grabbed the salad and dug in. "So good," I said around a mouthful.

"Clearly you're conflicted about this gift from your beloved," Tim said, taking a bite of a chocolate peanut butter cookie with a moan that was positively pornographic. After he finished chewing, he continued. "I don't have such feelings. Aidan just jumped up a few points in my book because I'm assuming you aren't eating all this, so I'm going to do you a favor and share with you."

"Oh, he asked me to bring your favorite wrap," Allyson said, turning the wraps over to read the labels. "Here you go," she handed one to him.

Tim took it, read the label, then looked at me. "Your man got me my fajita-chicken wrap."

"Of course he did," I said with a headshake. "You've gotten that every time we've eaten at the Sanctuary together and once made up an ode to it that you sang on top of a table at the brewery."

Tim rolled his eyes. "One, it was a low coffee table. It wasn't like I was on a high-top."

"Still," I murmured to Allyson's laughter.

"And two, I think Aidan has been there with us for two meals and the time I sang the song."

"You make an impression, Timmy," I said with a grin, wiggling my eyebrows at him. "It's no big deal. Aidan knew you were here with me."

Tim's face grew serious, which was a touch concerning. Leaning forward, he placed a hand on my arm, and I noted that his eyes were wet. "Gracie, as a gayer-than-gay teen who never thought he'd been accepted for how fabulous he was, it's never not a big deal when someone sees you, I mean really sees you. I hope you know what a keeper you've got."

I placed the salad on the table and walked up to Tim

and threw my arms around him. Squeezing him tight, I whispered, "Fuck those kids in your school that didn't get how amazing you were. You were so far from their orbit—they were simply looking at the stars."

"Damn right, chickie."

"You two." I looked over to see Allyson brush a tear away. "I didn't expect this, but I need to get out to the Woods. Holiday Glow is tonight at the park and the café is staying open late for anyone taking in the lights."

Highland Woods had begun Holiday Glow years ago, sponsored by some local businesses and institutions. They were lit up at night during the holidays, much like some zoos did in bigger cities. The park was always magical, but under white lights at Christmas, especially with a covering of snow, it was positively gorgeous.

"I hope you're getting a break for the holiday." I raised a brow at Allyson, coming to lean against the desk next to Tim and taking a breath after our moment. Looking closely at Allyson, I noted that even in her first trimester, she looked great. Last year she'd been spread so thin, trying to be there for both her cafés without adding staff, doing everything herself. Logan had helped her find some balance, and now they were married and going to have a baby.

She held up her hands, laughing. "Did Logan put you up to this questioning? Promise, I'm still rocking the balanced lifestyle. I had the morning off today to get in some yoga and just stopped by to grab a croissant for myself when we got Aidan's call. Only working this evening."

I stepped forward, enfolding my friend in a hug. "Proud of you."

She gave me a squeeze, then stepped back, scanning me from head to toe. I had gone more casual than usual for the library—an oversized green turtleneck sweater, distressed jeans, brown booties. "Girlie, you look more relaxed than I've seen you in ages."

"That's because she's getting some," Tim said with a mouthful of food.

"That'll do it." Allyson nodded sagely. With a more serious glance, she asked, "Any luck on daycare?"

I shrugged, trying not to despair because I'd felt so much lighter today as long as I didn't think about that one little issue. "Maggie has a call in to her provider. She heard a family was moving, but we haven't confirmed it."

"Lou is the source," Tim said as he moved on from the wrap to another cookie.

"Lou would know." Allyson nodded, considering.

"True, but just because someone is moving doesn't mean anytime soon. And it isn't like we're the only one looking for infant daycare. Cheryl had four infants, so I'd assume the other three families are desperate too."

"Well, I hope you get some positive news soon so you can enjoy the holiday," Allyson said with a squeeze of my hand.

"Thanks, hon. And thanks for bringing us this food. You really didn't have to."

"Oh, your husband can be very persuasive."

"That he can," I murmured as my phone chimed from the desk with a text.

"Oh girl, check this out," Tim said as he glanced at the small photo in the notification on my screen, holding it out to me.

With a tap to the screen, I opened the text and we all looked at the photo as it filled my screen. My husband and mother-in-law must have stopped by Highland Woods because the photo we were looking at was in the library at the mansion. Word on the street was that Logan hired a

Santa out there, though I was pretty sure it didn't start until later. I'd told Aidan we could skip the Santa photo op this year because I knew the line would be nuts that night. Somehow he apparently got in early since we were looking at the most adorable photo ever, taken from the side. Santa had an open-mouthed smile aimed at Mia, and she had the same shot back to him with her arms outstretched. My heart melted.

"Damn. If I had ovaries, they would have popped an egg at that cuteness," Tim said.

"Yeah, he really is one of the good ones," I whispered as I tapped out a reply. I waved bye to Allyson and nodded as Tim said he was going to do a lap, making sure the place was as cleaned up as we could be with another hour until close.

I sat at the desk, looking at the calendar on my phone. It was funny—just six days ago, the distance between Aidan and me had felt unsurmountable and was so tangible that it *hurt*. And now I knew we weren't completely back, but each moment we got closer. Sex was part of it, sure. Physical contact with him made me feel connected in a way that had been missing. But in seeing how he reacted to me, how he was aroused by me, I'd be lying if I said that wasn't a confidence boost.

It wasn't only Aidan that I'd been disconnected from. In getting our relationship back, I was returning to myself as well. I felt healthier in every part of my soul.

Now I just needed to figure out the daycare dilemma so I could stop stressing and enjoy the holiday. I was trying to make peace with a drive to Champaign every day. Ideal? No. Doable? I supposed. My phone chimed with another text.

Aidan: *Leaving the park to head home for a quick nap*

for the babe, and Mom is hitting the road so that she and Declan can come back down here on the 26th to celebrate with us then. Want to hit the Holiday Glow tonight with Mia for a walk in the lights? Shouldn't be too cold.

I loved this man to the depths of my soul. What I also realized was that I'd *missed him* in the past few months. I'd been so stressed, so out of my element, that I'd turned inward and shut everyone out, including him, all because mothering wasn't the easiest thing in the world and it rocked my confidence in myself. Enough of that bullshit, I was reclaiming what I wanted. That was Aidan and Mia. My friends. My job. Myself. I was done with staying home in case Mia cried and people thought I was a bad mom. Time to get my life back, one step at a time.

Me: *Sounds great. Give your mom another kiss from me and tell her thanks again. I'll be home in a little over an hour, and then we can hit the lights after we eat.*

Several hours later, I walked with my little family, winding through the lit trails of the park. There were Christmas lights strung over trees and bushes, wound around structures. The festive atmosphere had many visitors out at the park, whether they were taking a stroll on the path, enjoying carriage rides from the mansion, or standing around the bonfire in the meadow where a booth from the café was selling drinks for adults or hot chocolate for all. Allyson was also open indoors for people who wanted to warm up or grab a bite to eat.

Mia was snuggled into the sling at my chest but facing away from me, Baxter on his leash by Aidan. We'd realized as we started walking that Mia was absolutely mesmerized with the lights, just as she was with our Christmas tree at home, so we positioned her so she could see.

Every so often she'd coo and drop her head back to see

the lights, especially as we walked through the tunnel where you were surrounded with the warm white bulbs. As we reached the end, Aidan turned to wait for us, Baxter plopping to his butt and panting happily.

"You good, babe?" he asked, leaning forward and pressing a kiss to my temple.

I leaned in, inhaling the scent that I knew to be love. Mia was squeezed between us but seemingly very happy about that as she reached up and patted Aidan's face.

"I'm good. Great even." Looking up at the man I loved, I could see the boy he'd been. We'd been through so much in the past fifteen years. I couldn't wait to experience the next fifty with them.

"Hold on a second," he said, then tapped a teen who had just finished taking selfies with a friend. "Can I get you to take a pic of my family?"

"Sure!" She slid her own phone in her puffer vest and turned, assessing the lights and our stance. "Okay, get closer here and I can get the lights framing you all."

She stood back as we moved into position. She and her friend looked at the screen, positioning the phone a few different ways as she tapped it.

Faster than I could have even opened the app, she handed it back to Aidan. "There you go. I took several."

We called out thanks as she and her friend headed down the lit path to the Sunken Gardens, talking a mile a minute. Clearly the girl knew her stuff and was confident in her shot.

"Pretty good," Aidan murmured, showing me one of the pictures.

It made my breath catch. It was an intimate picture, that's the only way I could think to describe it. Aidan's arms were around us, his face pressed up to mine. She'd stepped back enough that Baxter was captured as well. The lights bathed us in a warm glow, and I freaking loved it.

"Let me get one of the two of you," Aidan said, stepping back.

I pressed a kiss to Mia's head as I looked Aidan's way. He took a picture, then lowered the phone, his warm brown eyes locked on mine. Without words, he stepped toward me, never breaking the gaze.

When he reached us, I whispered, "We can't drop down and go for it here, you know."

He shut his eyes then, shaking his head at me with a relaxed smile on his face. Looking at me once again, he dropped his mouth to my ear. "That's for later. For now I just need you to know how sexy you are."

I felt the heat warm my face. "Thanks?"

He stepped back, then wrapped an arm around me and started toward the café where we'd told Allyson and Logan we would swing by before heading home. "I just wanted you to know it. My mom pointed out that I had no pictures of you and Mia together, though you've taken several of me with her. I wasn't sure if it was because you didn't like the way you looked or something else, but my aim is to remedy that."

I thought about that for a minute as we passed a group setting off on the trail. Surely I'd taken some photos of me with Mia even if I hadn't asked Aidan to. Without speaking, I pulled my phone out, flipping through the pictures in my camera roll while I patted Mia on the butt, moving around a group of teens.

Coming to the day of her birth, I found one in the hospital. One. Interesting.

"Penny for your thoughts?" Aidan whispered as we

passed the pond at the mansion. Once we reached the door, he held it to let us inside.

"Thinking," I murmured. I headed immediately to some armchairs near the window. Allyson was fine with Baxter inside as long as we stayed away from the kitchen. Baxter was not a "let's go on a hike" kind of pup, so our leisurely stroll had tuckered him out and he collapsed near the chair that I lowered into.

Aidan paused next to me. "Want a drink?"

I looked from him to Allyson. "Hot chocolate?"

"Make that two," Aidan said.

Allyson nodded and got to work as Aidan tugged Mia from the sling, quickly checking her diaper before sitting down in the armchair next to me. He put his feet on the worn barnwood coffee table, letting Mia recline back against his thighs as he played with her feet.

I watched him for a moment or two. He was such a good dad. From some distance, I could see that I'd been jealous of the ease with which he'd slid into the role, not to mention how he didn't physically change as a result of it.

"I think I lost myself a little in the past year."

Aidan stopped looking at Mia to focus on me. He didn't say anything, just waited patiently for me to continue.

"I mentioned some of it the other night, but it's like there's so much I didn't even realize, like the pictures. Now that you mention it though, I can see what you're talking about." I looked down at my hands, twisting them because I didn't know what to do. Letting out a deep breath, I pulled my feet up to sit cross-legged, then continued. "It wasn't conscious, and I'm sure I wasn't in pictures by my choice, but also—and I don't mean to place blame—but you didn't take any of me either. I saw you with Mia and thought you two were adorable and took the picture. I know at times I realized you weren't doing the same, and if I'm being super honest here, I felt like it was just more evidence that you weren't attracted to me right now."

Aidan started to speak, but I put up a hand. "Give me a second to get this out. Now I'm aware that you're attracted to me, even in this new shape. I probably knew it deep down before, but it was like my very foundation was shaken."

Allyson quietly dropped the hot chocolates on our table and walked away, sensing, I'm sure, that we were in a heavy conversation.

Aidan continued to bicycle Mia's legs while watching me, so I went ahead and wrapped it up. "I'm glad we've started talking again, and I can't explain why I stopped except to say that I'd wanted for so long to be a mom that when I felt like I wasn't getting it right, when I wasn't feeling good about myself, I just started to turn inward and shut you out. I'm sorry, and I promise to talk more if I ever feel like that's happening again."

He dropped Mia's legs and pulled her to rest on his chest as he looked my way. "I'm good to speak?"

I rolled my eyes at him, gesturing for him to go ahead.

"I said this the other night and I'm repeating it again, but I'm so damn sorry I didn't notice everything you were struggling with. Society absolutely puts unfair pressure on moms and that's on all of us, but *I* should have seen you. I think I just got caught up in the day-to-day and missed it. But no more. We're communicating—in the bedroom and out. And you need to know and trust that I love the fuck out of you, Gracie."

I gave him a smirk. "You mean you're wrapped up in me."

He shook his head at me as he pulled back to look at our daughter. "Mia, I say a cheesy romance line *one time* and your mom won't let me live it down. And I'd like to note, it was *wrapped up in us.* As in, wrapped up in you two."

I unfolded my legs and leaned over to kiss first Aidan, then Mia. Sitting on the arm of his chair, I ran my hand through his hair. "You trying to tell me we have you wrapped around our fingers?"

Aidan looked up at me, resting his head against my chest. "Babe, you have no idea. I'm yours, your mine, and I don't care where we begin or end as long as we're in this together."

I laid my head on top of his. "Sounds good to me."

Chapter 14

Christmas Eve

A*idan*

I woke early, letting Baxter out and checking on Mia. She'd been sleeping like a rock star since the day we noticed she'd begun teething. That seemed counterintuitive—that should have shepherded in terrible sleep—but maybe since she was already sleeping terribly, we reversed the norm? Part of me also wondered if she'd been sensing Grace's stress and with it slowly dissipating, maybe she was settling as well? Whatever it was, I wasn't questioning six hours of sleep straight each night.

Mia was still zonked, so I got to work in the kitchen on my own. We'd returned from the Holiday Glow last night to put Mia down and soak in some time with each other. Can't say I was mad about that. With my mom gone and Mia sleeping, we'd been able to take our time with each other in a way I don't think we had for some time. It was like being with each other for years had given us a shorthand to knowing what we each liked and just going with what was comfortable and getting there quickly. Last night I spent time worshipping her body many times over. Surely that would help her to see that I loved her as she was, that I was attracted to her now and would be forevermore.

And was that the reason she was still snoozing long after dawn? I mean, I wouldn't deny it made me feel pretty damn good.

On the kitchen counter, I pulled together the ingredients for buttermilk pancakes. I looked forward to Mia being older and able to eat food. My mom had so many special recipes when we were growing up—making them for Mia would mean a lot. But for now I'd settle for taking care of her mom.

I synced my phone with the speaker in the kitchen, keeping the volume low enough not to wake anyone else. The sounds of Chris Stapleton filled the kitchen as I prepared the batter. Our fireplace was pumping out some warmth; the Christmas tree was lit up in the corner. Mom had helped wrap the gifts we'd purchased so Grace and I wouldn't have to stay up late doing that. The stockings were filled for the most part. All we had stretching ahead of us for the next two days was relaxing and spending time together, just the three of us.

My phone buzzed on the counter. I saw a missed message from my mom, but the new one was from Levi. I paused, skipping back to Mom's message. She was just checking on what she was bringing down on Saturday. We'd decided for this year to celebrate the actual holiday with only the three of us. With Declan's schedule, it worked best to celebrate on the weekend anyway, so we were gathering on the twenty-sixth.

Shooting off a text back to her, I then returned to Levi's message.

Levi: *You talk to Grace yet?*

Patience, it seemed, was not his friend. I thought back to

my conversation with Levi last night at the café in the park. He, Logan, and Maeve, had come in to see Allyson when she got off. The dynamic between Levi and Maeve was either going to blow up and we would all experience the shrapnel, or the two of them were going to make fireworks of their own. Time would tell.

Levi had made a comment to me again about how he was drowning in work before he left that had gotten me thinking. This morning I'd fired off an idea to him that he'd jumped on, but I couldn't commit until I talked to Grace.

Maggie had texted us as we visited at the café last night. The Harper family was officially moving, and we could snag their spot for an infant. But kicker was, they were moving in June.

Grace had taken it in stride. She said we could just deal with the inconvenience of driving to Champaign daily for half a year and had sent a quick message to Kris asking for the spot. She was right—commuting for the spring was a possibility. But I thought I had one that was even better.

Before I could put the pancakes on the griddle, I heard the telltale signs of Mia waking up through the baby monitor. Before I could leave my post, I heard Grace talking to her and assumed they'd be down shortly. I made quick work of making some decaf coffee and fed Baxter. I'd make the pancakes after she fed Mia. A slow start was likely perfect. Hell, if we didn't want to leave our pajamas, that worked.

As I waited for my family to make it to the kitchen, I wondered what our lives would be like in a few years. Five? Ten? This year Mia wouldn't even realize it was a holiday. When would that change? We wanted more kids, but who knew when that would happen?

Yesterday Mia and I'd had lunch with my mom before she headed home. She'd reminded me how important it was to soak in every moment. Mom wasn't overly senti-mental, but she'd teared up for a moment before squeezing my hand and saying how she remembered my first Christmas. I knew she was also thinking about my dad.

Having lost a parent at a young age, the notion of trea-suring each day had already been part of my DNA, but Mom's comment had stuck with me the day before. It was likely what inspired me to text Levi that morning.

Grace's voice through the monitor pulled me away from memories of the past and thoughts of the future. She was telling Mia that Santa would be coming down the chimney tonight. I shook my head with a laugh. Got to start them young, I supposed.

"And Mia, we're going to watch Mommy's favorite Christmas movie," Grace said as she moved into the kitchen. The way her face, and Mia's, lit up when they saw me was the best gift I'd ever received.

I crossed to them, holding out my arms for Mia as I pressed a quick kiss to Grace's lips. Stepping back and holding our little peanut to my chest, I gave Gracie a haughty look. "And the best Christmas movie is..."

"*Christmas Eve on Sesame Street* of course."

This was a familiar conversation. "That movie is easily ten years older than you."

"It was on every year, and with parents that were in education, there were only so many things I was allowed to watch. PBS was always on the approved list." Grace moved over to the coffee maker as she poured a mug and gave me a look filled with pity. "I'm so sorry that you lived a childhood without having Kermit trying to figure out how Santa was going to get down the chimney, but it is by far the best holiday movie." She leaned back against the counter, cupping both hands around her coffee mug as she took a sip and waited, knowing what was coming.

I gave her a headshake, my smile wide. We'd had this debate for years. "*A Christmas Story* is the ultimate. Your little *Sesame Street* show can't even compete. How can it when we have leg lamps and the Bumpuses' dogs?" I whispered loudly to Mia so that Grace would be sure to overhear. "Mia, I will educate you on all good movies. Your mommy isn't to be trusted here."

"Hey now, mister. You better watch it," Grace said, laughter lighting up her eyes. She moved her coffee to her side and hopped up on the counter before picking up the mug again. "So pancakes today?"

I kept my eyes locked on hers, wanting to make sure I didn't miss anything if she tried to mask any feeling beyond relief and joy. I didn't think she would, but after we'd made all these gains, I wasn't chancing anything. "Pancakes. I thought we might celebrate."

Her brows drew together. "Celebrate? What are we celebrating? Mia's first Christmas?"

"Or a possible solution to the daycare dilemma?"

She put her mug down and held her hands out for Mia, so I passed her over. "Well, yeah, I'll admit it is a relief that we can get her into Farm School this summer. Not thrilled about the daily drive, but maybe we can alternate?"

"Or"—I took a step to be between her legs and ran my hands over the crazily patterned pajama pants—"I could switch jobs and work from home part-time, keeping Mia with me until this summer?"

Grace froze, her eyes locking on mine. When she spoke, her voice was barely audible. "I'm sorry, Aidan, what? What would you do?"

"Actually use some of what I studied in college?" I

pressed a kiss to her mouth. "Levi has been working in free-lance video editing and a little web design for years. In the past few, he's been turning clients away because he simply can't do all the work. After talking to him last night, something was nagging at me and I thought of it this morning. I could work for him, part-time for now. We wouldn't feel the loss of income as much, and we already have benefits through your job, so that's not an issue. This summer Mia could start at Farm School, and I could move to full time as long as Levi and I both feel like it's a good fit."

"And you think Levi will be good with this?"

"I know he will. I texted him this morning to see. I didn't want to get your hopes up if he didn't have enough work."

Grace stared at me, her eyes wide. I didn't notice any concern, but I struggled to figure out what was there until she burst into tears and collapsed on me, Mia squashed between us as she protested in a baby squeak.

"Babe, you okay?"

"Aidan, this is perfect." She took a calming breath, then another. Pulling back, I saw her steady herself. "You really want this?"

I tucked a lock of her hair behind her ear and lowered my face to hers. "Baby, I'm positive. I'd love to stay home with Mia this spring. I can work a few hours a day here and there—when she's napping, when you're home."

"And you won't miss the sheriff's department?" Her blue eyes were endless pools of concern, not for what I was suggesting but that I was giving up too much.

"I'm not moving to Mars. I'll miss the guys, not the job, and they're still here. And have to say, the hours are an improvement."

She worried her lower lip under her teeth, seeming to

give that some consideration. "So you'll stay home this spring and then Mia will start Farm School and you'll work from home."

I nodded, watching, waiting.

She took a deep breath, let it out. "That's perfect."

"Kind of like you?" I winked.

She dropped her head to my shoulder. "Thanks for seeing the best part of me."

"Always, Grace-alicious," I whispered, tipping her chin up to meet my gaze. "Love you lots."

Her smile reached her eyes. "Love you more."

She had no idea. That wasn't even possible. I loved this woman to the depths of my soul. However, our daughter had a different plan for the day than her parents sharing their feelings on a counter in the kitchen. Mia let out a hungry cry to let us both know she was done with this.

"Well, I guess the princess has spoken," Grace said.

"Hop down—I'll help you get situated." I stepped back, taking Mia with me, as Grace got down. Within minutes, she and Mia were curled up on the couch under the lights of the tree. Baxter danced around my feet, chasing a ball he threw to himself.

I poured the batter onto the griddle, listening to Gracie singing "Starting Over" to Mia as she swayed while they nursed. I couldn't imagine a better life.

Epilogue

Merry Christmas

Grace

We'd been up for two hours. While I had grown to respect this new body of mine, especially with the way Aidan had been showing his own appreciation for it, I wasn't going to love the new size it would be if I continued to eat the way we had the day before with no exercise. Unless you counted sex as exercise. I was sure Aidan would, so I hadn't even asked. The new year would bring balance.

The menu consisted of an egg casserole and Aidan's mom's Christmas morning cinnamon rolls. On the plus side, we really didn't need to have lunch. On the negative, there were only two of us in this house who ate solid food—I wasn't counting the pup—and I wanted to eat every roll. I was working hard on self-control, and it wasn't looking good for my waistline.

Mia was doing some tummy time on a blanket under the tree, the scent of the Fraser fir still filling the room weeks after we'd gotten it. Sophia had warned us not to get Mia too many toys this year, and my parents had concurred.

They said she wouldn't remember anything. As a result, I'd gone with a set of pajamas, a book, and two toys. She really liked the mirror that dangled on her activity mat, so I got her a larger mirror for tummy time and a soft fish that had different fabrics to appeal to her senses. Currently she was checking out her reflection while she gnawed on the fish. Perfect.

Aidan was in the kitchen, cleaning up from breakfast as the windows to the backyard were filled with falling snow. He'd already checked the weather reports—we were supposed to get two to four inches by the end of the day. Enough to make it feel like the holiday, not enough to keep his family from coming down tomorrow. We'd already had a video call with them this morning and one with my parents. I wouldn't see them for the holiday, but we'd get together sometime in the new year.

"Hey babe," I called in. "Can you put on the Harry Connick Jr. Christmas album?"

"You bet!"

The first notes of "Sleigh Ride" flowed out of the speakers as Aidan left the kitchen and came to the living room, joining Mia and me on the floor. Baxter was preoccupied in the other corner with the only gift he really needed or even wanted—a Kong stocked with peanut butter and a treat to make him work for it.

Aidan scooted closer to me on the rug, putting a leg on either side of my hips, and I settled back against his chest, soaking in this moment that was everything I'd hoped for all those months and years ago. I wished I could go back and tell myself to relax, that the feeling of competence in parenting would come, but I wouldn't have believed it.

Heck, Sophia and I'd talked late in the night her last night here. She reminded me that the joy of parenting was figuring out how to be okay with the ups and downs, that as soon as you thought you had that age down, they'd grow and new issues would come. Find a way to enjoy the ride, she'd advised. Maybe I should get that tattooed on my forearm.

I looked from our baby to the winter wonderland outside. Today was simply perfection. As Mia babbled to herself in the mirror, Aidan slid another package on my lap. I looked down, then over my shoulder at him.

"What is this? We already exchanged gifts." I'd gotten him a Solo Stove. I'd thought it would be a good gift, so I'd ordered one during the Black Friday sale. After seeing how he enjoyed it at Logan's the other night, I'd patted myself on the back for my forward thinking, betting he would love it, and he sure had.

He'd surprised me with earrings from Caitlin, a jeweler in town. They were beautiful, and I had zero desire to take them off. He'd also scheduled a hair appointment with my stylist over break. It might have made me cry; I was so ready.

"Your earrings were your big gift; this is just a small thing." He slid an arm around my stomach, resting his chin on my shoulder as he kissed my neck. "Open it."

"Stubborn man," I grumbled, tearing the paper open to see the backside of a picture frame. I flipped it over to see a picture of Mia and me framed in silver. My breath caught as I fought back a wave of emotions. We were in our bedroom upstairs. If I wasn't mistaken, this was from a few nights ago, maybe the night after we'd talked and reconnected? Mia was lying sideways across my lap, nursing as she always did at the beginning where she'd look up at me as much as she could, one hand either on my face or reaching for me. I was looking at her with a love that took my breath away.

It was beautiful. We were beautiful.

A tear fell down my cheek. Then another.

"Do you see it?" Aidan whispered. "Do you? Mia is the luckiest girl on the planet, and I'm the luckiest guy because you made the decision to love us."

"I see it," I whispered. I dropped my head back to rest on his chest, his arms surrounding me and our baby playing nearby, our pup happily occupied, music filling the house, and a snow globe filling the morning sky. My life was so blessed.

Merry Christmas indeed.

Acknowledgments

This book is far more personal to me than any I've ever written. One thing I've learned in writing books is that by putting your writing out into the world, you invite readers to start asking how much of "you" is in your stories. I'm going to assume that it's different for every author. But for me, there's a lot.

Now, as a romance author I can assure you that those "spicy scenes" the guys talk about in this book are not from life. No, just no. Yikes. What does come from my life are phrases I overhear, locations in my town, and fears or dreams I might have myself. I give my characters my favorite songs, food I love, and sometimes a media lounger I want to buy for my house.

In this book I gave Grace my struggles as a mom in those first few months of my oldest son's life.

I cannot remember a time in my life I didn't want to be a mom. I'll say here that I absolutely don't think everyone needs to be a parent, I know plenty of people with full lives that aren't one. I also know that the path to becoming one can be fraught and my heart breaks for anyone that has that struggle. That being said, I've always wanted to be a mom and I was absolutely rocked with how my sense of self changed upon the birth of our oldest.

To be honest, I lost myself.

I still remember a colleague from school coming to drop off a dinner a month after our son was born. Melinda had looked from the baby sleeping peacefully to me and asked how long my husband and I had been married. I'd replied seven years. She nodded, said that had been the same for her, then squeezed my arm and said, "It will get easier, I promise."

She left and I burst into tears. I've never felt more isolated in my life as I had those first few months. Her words gave me the acknowledgement that I wasn't alone.

I wanted Grace to give voice to the struggles many of us face in the first months of parenthood. We don't want to be ungrateful, but it's a shock to the system. Like Grace, I love my children with every fiber of my being. Also like Grace, I had zero desire to stay home full time with them, even if I could have. I wish for all new moms friends like Emma and Maggie. Mother-in-laws like Sophia. Husbands like Aidan. And I send out sparkly fairy dust into the universe to everyone in the hopes that you learn to love yourself as your perfectly imperfect selves. You are beautiful just as you are.

Xoxo,

Kat

About the Author

Kat Ryan is a middle school teacher by day and a budding romance author in the free time she steals for herself. She loves to write about small towns, found families, strong women, and cinnamon roll heroes that love them. She's a sucker for a HEA and more than a bit of steam in the stories she writes.

Kat lives in the Midwest with her husband and her two sons where she consumes a steady diet of coffee, chocolate, and romance books. And while her students and sons plan to never read the books she writes, her husband has and continues to cheer her on.

Want more from Grace and Aidan? Subscribe to Kat's newsletter on her website, https://katryanwrites.com. All "extras" for each of Kat's book are linked in the newsletter that comes out every month.

Also by Kat Ryan

Coming Home - Max and Emma

Finding Beauty - Sully and Maggie

Loving Ivy - Jake and Ivy

Follow Your Dreams - Nate and Elle

Starting Over - Drew and Kate

Running on Empty - Logan and Allyson

www.ingramcontent.com/pod-product-compliance
Lightning Source LLC
Chambersburg PA
CBHW031542310726
48971CB00008B/2596